Vossoff
Nim...

Just a Couple of Idiots Reupholstering Space and Time

Other books by Adam-Troy Castro

Fiction
Lost in Booth 9
   (1993, Silver Salamander)
Time's Arrow Book 2: The Present
   (1998, Berkeley Boulevard)
The Gathering of the Sinister Six
   (1999, Berkeley Boulevard)
A Desperate, Decaying Darkness
   (2000, Wildside Press)
An Alien Darkness
   (2000, Wildside Press)
The Revenge of the Sinister Six
   (2001, Ibooks)
The Secret of the Sinister Six
   (2002, Ibooks)

Vossoff and Nimmitz

Just a Couple of Idiots Reupholstering Space and Time

ADAM-TROY CASTRO

WILDSIDE PRESS
Doylestown, Pennsylvania

Copyright © 2002 Adam-Troy Castro.
All rights reserved.

Some of these stories have been altered since their original publications.

Vossoff and Nimmitz
An original publication of
Wildside Press
P.O. Box 301
Holicong, PA 18928-0301

www.wildsidepress.com

FIRST EDITION

*I never met him
but through him I met Arthur, Zaphod, Marvin, Trillian,
Zarniwoop,
the Vogons,
a plummeting sperm whale
a planet inhabited by professional telephone sanitizers
and a universe that makes almost as much sense as this one.
This one's for Douglas Adams.*

Table of Contents

Just a Couple of Outrageous Lies
About the Illegitimate Son of Sid Caesar
and Imogene Coca 9
    an Introduction by Scott Edelman

Prologue 15

Just a Couple of Sentients
Sitting Around Talking. 25

Just a Couple of Extinct Aliens
Riding Around in a Limo 39

Just a Couple of Space Rogues
Playing Name That Tune 55

Interlude One. 71

Just a Couple of Pastrami Sandwiches
in a Living Room the Size of Infinity. 73

Interlude Two 91

Just a Couple of Highly Experimental Weapons Tucked
Away Behind the Toilet Paper 93

Just a Couple of Freelance Strikebreakers
Arguing Economics in the Liver of Justice 119

Just a Couple of Subversive Alien Warmongers
Floating All Alone in the Night 153

*Just a Couple of Ruthless Interstellar Assassins
Discussing Real Estate Investments
at a Twister Game the Size of a Planet* 181

Epilogue 219

A Ridiculously Lengthy Afterword 223

Just a Couple of Outrageous Lies About the Illegitimate Son of Sid Caesar and Imogene Coca
An Introduction by Scott Edelman

Having to take the stage (even one that's only made of paper and ink) before Adam-Troy Castro is a very daunting thing. I imagine that it's a bit like opening for Robin Williams. Readers who've plunked down their hard-earned simoleans for a collection of humorous stories written by the guru of the gut-busting guffaw and starring those inept space criminals Vossoff and Nimmitz will have little patience for the introduction that comes between them and the tales, since those who have even the least familiarity with the author or subject matter will know in their bones that nothing I have to say could possibly seem funny compared to what will follow.

You see, in the *Hollywood Squares* of comedic SF, Adam-Troy Castro occupies the center square. The rest of us are just lucky to be allowed to share the board from time to time.

So I'm just going to play this straight, since every comedian needs a straight man (though Adam, if he wished, could do without one, and play the roles of comic, straight man, heckler and laugh track all rolled into one). He is the king of the kibitzers.

So let me segue to the meat of the matter with an old comedic standby.

But seriously, folks.

I consider myself to have been raised by the Muse of Comedy.

Suckled at the boob tube, I learned all I know about office dynamics from *The Dick Van Dyke Show* and *The Mary Tyler Moore Show*, all I know about friendship from *The Honeymooners* and *The Abbott and Costello Show*, and all I know about love and marriage from *I Love Lucy* and *The Addams Family*.

When my parents made us turn from the sitcoms to watch variety programs such as *The Ed Sullivan Show* or *The Jackie Gleason Show*, I'd zone out for most of the hour, ignoring the plate-spinners, the dancing bears, and even the dancing girls. (Hey, I was young!) Those types of entertainers seemed artificial. I knew they had little to teach me. Only the comedians could get to the heart of the matter. They seemed to know the secrets of life. They were the philosophers who taught me how best to wend my way through the universe. Alan King. Henny Youngman. Jackie Vernon. Totie Fields. Jackie Mason. Rodney Dangerfield. George Carlin. They spoke the truth and made me laugh. I took their jokes as my gospel, memorizing them for later, usually waiting to share what I had learned until I was in the middle of a class, whispering shaggy dog stories into the ears of my fellow third graders at the worst possible moments, inevitably earning a visit to the principal's office.

But it was always worth it. For comedy was magic, and making people laugh was a form of alchemy.

As I grew, new sitcoms and a younger generation of comedians came into my life, but the old fascination with humor always remained.

So I've heard all them all, every variation, and even when I'm listening to the rare ones that I haven't heard before, I can see through to the skeleton of the joke clearly as it's being laid out before me. I'm not an easy mark. I can see the punch lines coming. In fact, I can even see the set-ups coming, and so sometimes, when faced with a particularly uncreative comic, I will say the punchline aloud before it arrives, usually to the surprise and dismay of my wife, who still wonders, "How did you know he was going to say that?"

When you've been so totally immersed as I have in standup and sitcom for an entire lifetime, the invisible becomes visible, and the blueprints of most jokes become obvious.

I can't help it.

That's why it isn't an easy thing to get me to laugh.

But Adam-Troy Castro can make me laugh.

Out loud. Repeatedly. Painfully. In a manner known to cause tears. His jokes, approaching like ninjas, are able to sneak up on me before my defenses have time to pop up.

Miraculously, he doesn't even have to be there. He can do it with the magic of his words on the page.

Adam-Troy Castro's history with the late, lamented (and if I may be allowed an angry aside, *damn* the fact that I have to call it that) *Science Fiction Age* was a long one. He was present at the creation. As editor, I can think of no other piece of fiction more suited to have been the first story in my first issue than "The Last Robot." (Which you'll not find here, as rather than being funny, it was a tender farewell to the late Isaac Asimov, who had just been lost to us. You'll have to seek out that tale in his short-story collection *An Alien Darkness*.) I've reread "The Last Robot" many times since I first chose to publish it, and it has continued to move me each time. But as skilled a creation as "The Last Robot" was, it gave me no hint of the madness that was to follow, a bit of orchestrated insanity that arrived camouflaged in a manila envelope under the title "Just a Couple of Sentients Sitting Around Talking."

Now, before we go on, there's one thing you must understand. Over the years, I had read many stories submitted to *Science Fiction Age* by writers who thought they were funny, but very few by writers who actually *were* funny. Comedy is not an easy endeavor, and SF comedy is even harder than that. But Castro's tale of bumbling crooks tripping over each other across the galaxy had me in stitches, and seemed the perfect complement to the oftentimes dark stories I was publishing. So I bought that first Vossoff and Nimmitz story (not yet realizing that it *was* the first), and it eventually appeared in the September 1994 issue, with a marvelous illustration by Joel F. Naprstek, who went on to do the illustrations for all future Vossoff and Nimmitz tales. And that, I thought, was the end of that.

It had seemed a harmless enough editorial decision. But then Adam showed me that I had underestimated him. Another manila envelope arrived, one that seemed equally as innocuous as had the first, this one containing "Just a Couple of Extinct Aliens Riding Around in a Limo," and I suddenly realized to my horror that I was responsible for unleashing a comedic cancer on the world.

When I chose to publish that first Vossoff and Nimmitz story, I did not dream it would start a series. In fact, if I had realized what was about to occur, what that nefarious literary mastermind Adam-Troy Castro was attempting to do, I might have resisted publishing that first tale, no matter how much it had made me laugh. See, I don't particularly like series. I believe a story should have a beginning and a middle and an end, and not a beginning and a middle and then another middle and then still yet a further middle, which is what series really are. Most sequels diminish the luster of the original, and are to be ignored.

So when I received the second story featuring the same two lunkheads, I was leery. I felt prejudiced against it before I even started reading. As soon as I saw the crime being perpetrated, I wanted an excuse to reject the manuscript. But see, to do that, I had to actually read it. Which meant that I couldn't find any such excuses.

Why?

Because he was able to make me laugh, and for that I'll forgive just about anything. The second story was even funnier than the first, and I was won over. I was seduced by the funnybone of Adam-Troy Castro. (And there's a *True Confessions* story title for you!) I won't try to explicate his humor here. I won't tell you why or where I laughed, because nothing is as unfunny as a joke telegraphed. I want you to laugh as I did, discovering the comedic landmines for yourself.

What can I say? I was weak. "Just a Couple of Extinct Aliens Riding Around in a Limo" was published in the January 1995 issue, which was a mistake, because it only encouraged him.

From that moment on, as soon as I published one Vossoff and Nimmitz story, another arrived. I had consecutive Vossoff and Nimmitz stories in my inventory from that day on until *Science Fiction* Age died. In fact, the final story you'll read in this volume was sitting on my desk the day Sovereign Media decided to axe the title. So not only was Adam-Troy Castro there before the beginning, he was also there after the end. Mailing that story back to Adam, instead of the contract he deserved, was one of my saddest duties as editor.

But you're in luck. You get to read it now, capping off all the others.

And beware. Because though this volume contains all the Vossoff and Nimmitz stories currently written, Adam-Troy Castro is still out there. He is on the loose. He has a sense of humor, and he isn't afraid to use it.

Wherever a joke is in need of a punchline, he'll be there. Wherever a face is yearning for a collision with a Boston cream pie, he'll be there. And wherever an editor needs to laugh hard enough that he passes an entire roast beef sandwich through his nose, he'll be there.

So before you turn the page to begin experiencing what you *really* plunked down your dollars for, put down that soda, unless you want to find your shirtfront soon soaked. Send away all small children, lest the sound of a grown person alternately laughing and weeping warp their tender minds. And whatever else you do, remember —

Should an innocent-seeming manila envelope arrive in your mailbox, don't open it.

You've been warned.

Scott Edelman has been nominated four times for the Hugo Award in the category of Best Editor, primarily due to his acumen in publishing the works of Adam-Troy Castro. His short-story collection, These Words Are Haunted, *is currently available from Wildside Press.*

Prologue

Somewhere beyond the stars, well past the scattered light of the unknown universe, in a realm so distant that no life of any kind has ever ventured there, and where the fundamental rules of time and space have never applied, there's nothing.

If you find yourself in such a place, you know you've gone too far.

Closer in, there's interesting stuff.

There's Hotworld, a civilization suffering beneath the heel of another who they happened to piss off for reasons lost to history. Their tormentors, who are not nice people in general, wrapped a string of unbreakable but elastic neutronium around a groove they excavated in the planet's equator. This they connected to a fixed mass-driver of unparalleled power which alternately propels their world toward the sun, then yanks it back whenever the string has unspooled as far as it will go. Hotworld, which is now essentially a giant inhabited yo-yo, oscillates back and forth toward its sun for all eternity, its distance to that orb ranging from approximately that of Venus to approximately that of Mars, a condition which requires its busy population to live in cities on wheels that must constantly travel first north and then south to escape the seasonal weather extremes at either latitude — a lifestyle which is difficult enough when the artificial intelligence controlling their planet's plight doesn't decide it wants to Walk the Dog.

Not a nice place.

There's also Pollenworld, a planet universally allergenic to anybody unlucky enough to land upon it. Its atmosphere is gray with blobs of fluffy shmootz so clearly the sworn enemy of every being with nasal passages that just to look upon it, from orbit perhaps, causes fits of uncontrollable sneezing that leave streaks on navigation panels and utterly ruin the dignity of starship captains. The forces of evolution attempted to compensate by producing life forms that were essentially nothing but cavernous nasal passages with feet, in the theory that creatures with nostrils the size of hula hoops wouldn't find themselves irritated by allergens; this, alas, failed to work, and the sentient creatures doomed to life upon its surface were forced to develop a planetary civilization with a culture entirely devoted to nonstop honking at each other. Evolution, which is well known as a wacky beast, attempted to take pity on them by pinching their humongous nostrils shut on both ends, a solution which didn't stop them from feeling the need to sneeze but which did change their planetary culture to one entirely based on great gobs of brain matter backfiring out the tops of their heads. They are certainly one species with a bone to pick with the tissue of space-time.

Also: not a nice place.

Finally, there's Mouthworld, not so much a planet as an advanced organism the size of a planet, lined from pole to pole with literally billions of sharply-fanged mouths. One would expect that if you landed on this planet you would take one step away from your rocket-shaped spaceship only to feel a sudden violent jerk as a forked tongue snaked from one of those mouths, whipped around your torso, snapped your spine, and dragged you screaming toward the slavering, salivating fangs of the nearest toothy fissure; that you would draw your blaster from its belt-hoster and fire zap after zap of superheated plasma at the gaping maw, screaming die die die as the teeth, impervious to your fire, merely snapped together hungrily in expectation of the fine treat to come. You would think that, but it's not what happens. In actuality, Mouthworld would starve to death if it needed unwary space travellers for sustenance. It lives off starlight. The mouths aren't there to devour you, but to criticize you, saying all sorts of nasty things about your dayglo orange jumpsuit or wondering why it's been so long since you called your Mom. Travellers who break down on Mouthworld tend to use the blasters on themselves rather than bear yet another warning not to slouch.

None of them, nice places.

And then there's one more place, which is particularly Not Nice.

Any guide directing travellers to the notable sites of the universe (and yes, you can include that one, if you want, as long as you don't bring it up here; jesus, we're sick of hearing it mentioned, already) includes a compendium of the sleaziest and most appalling bars in all of space-time. This is usually intended to aid the unwary in avoiding such places, but you never know; sometimes people seek out the bottom of the barrel deliberately, in the apparent belief that the monkeys who previously occupied that receptacle left some Cartier or Tiffany jewelry somewhere in the cocktail of unpleasant and malodorous substances that always percolate to the bottom of any container left unwashed after its usage for the mass storage of chittering lower primates. (Also, some people are just plain sleazy themselves, and like anything best compared to bodily fluids just naturally like to seek out their own level.) In any event, whether you run screaming from such establishments in favor of fashionable fern-bars where the water costs more than the beer, or run leering toward them in search of undiscriminating members of your preferred sex and species who won't have any problem indulging the kink that gets you dropped down trap doors in all the respectable places, the ranking of sleaziest bars anywhere and anytime is a list that most guides assemble with the greatest possible diligence, using a variety of arcane scientific criteria ranging from the diversity of the communicable diseases to the number of wet hacking coughs each patron is permitted to spew before being denied access to the establishment's one communal napkin.

Narrow the list down to the hundred sleaziest, and you have a hundred places so sleazy that mere inhalation within their walls causes a degree of cranial fermentation that renders the actual drinking of alcohol redundant. Narrow the list down the fifty sleaziest, and you have fifty places so sleazy that even Batman would fear breaking through the skylight in search of stoolies he could beat up for information. Narrow the list down to the ten sleaziest, and at least seven of them will be places situated on the same strip of Patterson, New Jersey, in 1967. But use the process of elimination, selecting from that ten one bar so devoid of any redeeming feature, so absent the homey quality that allows these shrines to incipient alcoholism the pretense that they're friendly neighborhood hangouts where everybody knows your name, and you will find, out of all creation, in all of space and time, the tavern where you go only if your definition of drowning your sorrows includes the possibility of sinking over your head in the slime trails of all the previous drinkers who have been to that den of iniquity before you.

It's called Ralphs.

There is no apostrophe. It is not owned by anybody named Ralph. It uses the word the same way another famous bar, in another era, used the word Cheers. That place cheered; this place ralphs. It is situated in the worst neighborhood of the worst city on the worst planet of the worst solar system of the worst star cluster in the known universe; you cannot get there by accident, as in, let's say, taking the wrong exit out of hyperspace, pulling over next to the steaming mound of rubble a generous person would call a building and leaving your wife and kids in the vermin-laden swamp that is the closest thing Ralphs has to a parking lot so you can run inside and ask the scarred and glowering patrons whether they know the best way to Disney's new park on Orion. You have to try to get there, overcoming all the barriers an aghast and revolted universe is bound to place in your way, and the worst thing that can possibly be said about sentients who manage it is that they did so knowing fully well that once they arrived they would have nobody to associate with but a bar filled with other sentients who wanted the same thing.

Enter Ralphs and you'll find in place of a scowling bartender and array of liquor bottles a single massive mound of quivering flesh that serves both functions. A product of highly advanced genetic engineering, this creature (which has no name, but which is sometimes called Callahan), has an IQ somewhere in the lower single digits and a body chemistry that feeds on a combination of abuse and stale cigar smoke and excretes a substance identical to cheap whiskey. Anybody who wants a drink can simply swagger up to this pathetic beast, blow smoke in the sucking orifice it possesses instead of a face, call it the foulest name in his personal lexicon and nail it with a sucker punch. Hard liquor oozes from the point of impact. On busy nights the bar at Ralphs is crowded with a double line of thugs and misanthropes shouting obscenities at the top of whatever they have for lungs and wailing away at the blubbery invertebrate with both fists, while confederates dart in and out catching the effluent with any of the dozens of unwashed glasses that litter the surrounding floor to ankle-depth. On quiet nights the creature just sits there in a puddle of iridescent raw corn liquor, trembling as it waits for the abuse, the delicious nourishing abuse, to start again.

I told you the place was called Ralphs for a reason.

Then there's the jukebox, which is deliberately kept stocked with songs that everybody hates. It tends to stick on those particularly awful, playing them again and again and again and again while the aggravated patrons do things like set it or fire or encase it in cement. An indestructible creation of the Bettelhine Munitions Corporation, apparently intended to demoralize any planetary civilization less ridden with scum than this one, it never stops playing; it just selects another highlight from the career of Neil Diamond or Michael Bolton and revs up again, scarcely noticing when the aggravated cyborg at Table Four knocks it over with a surface-to-air missile. Sometimes it says "Ow."

But by far, the sleaziest and most pathetic element of a night at Ralphs is the regular discussion of those notorious interstellar rogues, Ernst Vossoff and Karl Nimmitz.

On the night we join them, the discussion was being led by a globular creature with one gigantic eye on a stalk; you could tell he was a pirate because that eye was covered with a patch, and he kept bumping into things. He squirted the jukebox with a noxious foul-smelling acid and said, "Arrrr. I knew those lubbers many a time, back when they were just starting out; made one entire run through the coal sack with me comet shield on the blink, so I suited 'em up, strapped 'em to the front of me starship, and gave them a couple of ice picks to take care of incoming traffic. Wasted many a genomat treatment growing them new bodies whenever they got smashed to atoms, but saved money by paying 'em minimum wage; and grateful they were to get it, too. Arrrr."

"I had a cousin who knew them," said another patron, this one a muscular and bulletproof alien in blue tights and red cape. He was in the midst of attempting to turn off the jukebox by slamming it repeatedly against the walls and ceiling. "He said they'd lost their latest starship on some expedition or another, and were earning money for a new one by standing on the big red X in a coin-op nuclear bombardment range. Little kids used to come in after school and fork over their lunch money for the pleasure of nuking the two most famous losers in the universe into hydrogen ions. Most of the money was taken by the arcade's management, of course, but poor Ernst and Karl still raked in twelve cents per vaporization. It probably took them a couple of thousand years just to buy their way out of their contract, but even so . . ."

"Annnnh, yer both full of arcturian noodles," muttered another patron, who joined in the fun by pelting the offending jukebox with olive pits from an endless supply he kept in his vest pocket for just that purpose. He was only half-involved in the discussion, being deeply engrossed in the single issue of *Anvil-Man Comics* that represented what was for him a lifetime's supply of reading matter; he tended to forget the storyline between perusals, and thus always reacted with supreme astonishment when the bad guy got smooshed flat by the hero's namesake weapon. "I met Ernst Vossoff years ago, before he hooked up with his idiot partner. He was the most formidable man I ever knew; he could reassemble a star drive faster than you could say Jack Robinson with your tongue tied behind your back. He spoke seventy interstellar languages, knew eighty forms of martial arts, and mixed a mean cocktail. If he ever fell on bad times — and I admit he did, frequently; folks just kept dropping those banana peels out their windows on any thoroughfare he chose to travel — it was because the universe just couldn't tolerate the one mind capable of bringing it down. There aren't any words for how deeply I admired him, how without reservation I pitied him, and how sorrowfully I had to hurl him out that airlock in hyperspace. He turned up alive again, of course; he always did. Wonder what happened to him?"

"Arrrr," said the eyestalked pirate, "Me too."

"And me three," said the spitcurled alien.

All three blasted the jukebox with incineration beams, just for emphasis, an act which made it glow red hot before its internal cooling system freed it to play yet another encore of "Stand by Your Man."

That's when the lady entered the establishment.

It was rare for a lady to cross the threshhold of Ralphs. Women, sure. Women are fully capable of being every bit as sleazy as men; they have to, in order to keep up. But ladies are another matter — let alone beautiful ladies. This creature was pure diamond-edged perfection; she had a face so radiant that the bartender immediately spewed pure Johnny Walker, a walk so sensual that the local volcanoes spewed carbon monoxide just to maintain the world's otherwise undisturbed awfulness, and red hair so sleek and shiny that any automobiles in the vicinity would have stopped under the mistaken assumption that they had just encountered a stop light. Her eyes would have been piercing if they had actually possessed cutting edges, but they were eyes and therefore didn't, thus making that an inappropriate and stupid adjective. There was not a right angle on her entire body, whatever that means. It would have been fair to also say that she had a pair of legs that just wouldn't quit, except that her ability to stop walking when she reached the jukebox would have proved that statement, too, a lie. She was Eden, Xanadu, Atlantis, El Dorado, Epcot. She was not just perfection, but the quintessence of perfection, redundant as that seems: paradise in human form.

The jukebox switched to the Mormon Tabernacle Choir version of "Louie, Louie." The lady grabbed it with both hands, lifted it high over her head, and slammed it hard against the barroom floor, imbedding it in the semi-liquid muck that appears on the floor of any bar sleazy enough to never see the business end of a mop. The impact resonated powerfully enough to register on seismographs. The jukebox said, "Ow," and switched to a sound effect record of monks hitting themselves over the head with boards. Satisfied, and flashing a seductive smile which immediately turned the knees of every sentient in the bar to goo — even those which, by natural phenotype, already were goo — she produced a long-stemmed champagne glass, sauntered over to the bartender, whispered something too soft and seductive for anything with merely human ears to discern, and received pure Dom Perignon in tribute. This she sipped daintily while marching past a room filled with the fainting and awestruck to take her rightful position at the table where the pirate alien, the spitcurled alien, and the alien with the comic book all sat gaping, their respective tongues dangling in the regularly-spaced grease spots that here served as the equivalent of checkered tablecloths.

She said: "You want to know about Ernst Vossoff and Karl Nimmitz? Not the made-up stories you've been regaling each other with, but the real thing? Their failures, their triumphs, their loves, their losses, and their ultimate fates?

You want to know what they were like, and where they are now?"

The silence in the bar was a physical thing, too big to be weighed and too acrid to be used as an ingredient for bread.

The eyestalked alien spoke for all of them. "Arrrrr."

"Then listen up," the beautiful woman said. "Because I'm the only one with the full story . . ."

Just a Couple of Sentients Sitting Around Talking

Their orbital mapping completed, Vossoff and Nimmitz found their first impression correct: with the possible exception of Earth itself, which ever since the overzealous redecorating binge of 2754 had been the planetary equivalent of a dentist's waiting room, Fylis VII had to be the single dullest inhabited place in the known universe.

There were no surface features whatsoever. There were no jungles filled with ravenous beasts locked in savage struggles for survival, no architecturally improbable mile-high spires left by vanished alien civilizations, and no optical-illusion canals to interest the crackpot population of the next inhabited planet over. There were no valleys or mountains, no oceans or ice caps or deserts, no volcanoes or fjords, no swamps or geysers or cliffs, no prairies or tundra, and not even any gently sloping hills, and let's face it, even the dullest solid planet has gently sloping hills, even if they're only a few inches high and therefore no good for tobogganing. But not Fyliss VII, the cueball planet, a smoothly-polished sphere with a white sky and a white landscape and a white horizon — a planet that all in all just didn't seem to have a point to it.

The ship's brain said that the planet was home to an ancient civilization of Beings Far More Advanced Than Man. That was all the ship's brain said; the rest of the entry was randomized gibberish. This was par for the course, as Nimmitz had stolen the memory systems from a street vendor.

Nimmitz scratched his head, which was smooth and hairless and therefore resembled Fyliss VII a lot more than he would have liked to admit. "Where's the ancient civilization of beings far more advanced than Man?"

"Well," replied Vossoff, instructing the computer to put the necessary graphic on-screen, "assigning this latitude here as the equator, and this here as the meridian, it's 34 degrees north, 53 degrees west. Where the x is."

"That's an advanced civilization? There's nothing there. Just a couple of sentients sitting around talking."

Vossoff regarded the magnified picture on the orbital cameras: an aerial shot of two hairless sexless bipeds busily chatting with each other. One of the bipeds was light grey, the other dark grey. The light one was on his hands and knees, forming a makeshift bench upon which the dark one sat. "Nobody said it was an exciting advanced civilization."

"I hope not. Sitting on each other like that."

"If they're as advanced as the Brain says, maybe we're not meant to understand it."

"Maybe they're the local village idiots and the truly advanced population is underground laughing at them. Sitting on each other like that."

"No. I've run a thorough density scan of the entire planet. There are no caves, no artifacts, no geological layering, not even a molten core. Sliced in half, this globe would be as homogenous as a baked potato. No, my friend. I'm afraid those two sentients, boring and undistinguished as they appear to be, are the entire fabled advanced civilization of Fyliss VII."

Nimmitz couldn't take his eyes off the little red x on the screen. "I don't think there's anything worth stealing here, Ernst. They don't even have chairs."

"They might have secrets," said Vossoff. "And they, my friend, are always worth looting."

They landed the starship just over the horizon from the fabled advanced civilization. It was a rough landing, as the starship was one of those inverted pyramid things that used to be all the rage among starfarers a few decades back, and while it looked nicely retro, it was also incredibly top-heavy. Vossoff and Nimmitz had a few tense moments when the ship started to tip, but managed to compensate by hastily shifting some crates of highly illegal stimulants in the cargo hold.

"Gotta get the stabilizers fixed," gasped Nimmitz.

"Make enough money on this trip," said Vossoff, "we won't have to." He jabbed his blaster into its holster. "Come on."

They descended the gangplank and began their cross-country trek toward the fabled advanced civilization of Fyliss IV. The walk was, as anybody could have predicted, a dull one. Anybody painting landscapes here could have produced them at the rate of ten a minute. The emptiness was so total that only men as coarse as Vossoff and Nimmitz could have failed to be terrified by it. But then, they were men who lived for the deal, the scam, the sting, the easy way to riches, the satisfaction of knowing they'd just screwed somebody out of something. They were men willing to rob and kill for a percentage point, but were really only good at getting screwed first.

They walked two kilometers, before their detail-starved eyes picked up a miniscule gray dot on the horizon ahead. As they approached, the gray dot resolved itself into the two hairless bipeds, who had shifted position since the Vossoff and Nimmitz spotted them from orbit: now the dark one provided the bench on which the lighter one sat. Both seemed utterly comfortable with this arrangement, which had evidently been going on for generations, as the bipeds had both evolved padded hands and knees.

Vossoff and Nimmitz approached to within several meters of the aliens, waiting in vain for the other shoe to drop. It didn't. If it was going to drop at all, it was one hell of a big shoe.

It was Nimmitz who broke the silence. "Fine way to be spending their days. Sitting on each other like that."

Vossoff fingered his walrus moustache contemplatively. "You should open your mind, my friend. Ever been to Phlaaaarg IX, home of the N'loghthi? They punctuate all their spoken sentences by hitting each other in the face with creamy pastries. Their planetary legislature looks like a road-show pie fight. Next to that, this is relatively normal."

"But why do they sit on each other like that?"

"I don't know. Maybe it's a mating ritual. Or maybe it's their religion. Or maybe —"

For the first time, the lighter alien took notice of them. "Or maybe," it said, in perfectly-accented Interlac, "we're just extremely civilized, that's all."

Nimmitz fell back a step and said, "Gaaaaaa."

Vossoff, who usually took surprises well, didn't sound much better. "You . . . understand us?"

"Oh," the lighter alien said, "we understand every known language. We don't get visitors often, but when we do, the planet itself translates for us. One of the many trans-dimensional mechanisms we've set up to support our lives here."

Nimmitz broke in: "Why do you take turns sitting on each other like that?"

"Isn't it obvious? We live on a planet with no chairs, and no resources to build chairs. Since we consider sitting on the ground barbaric, one of us must be a chair at all times. If we were not as civilized as we are, one of us would force the other to be the chair permanently, but we are an ancient and advanced race, and therefore we politely take turns."

"Without anything so crude as a monetary system," the darker alien amplified, "this is also as close as we come to having an economy."

"Yes," the lighter alien said. "Supply and demand."

Nimmitz was boggled. "And is that all you do all day? Sit on each other like that?"

"There is nothing else to do. So we spend our days sitting on each other and discussing philosophy. For instance, just as you showed up I was advancing the notion that causality is itself the root cause of most events —"

"— whereas I," the darker alien said, "take the opposing viewpoint, that there can't possibly be any such thing as causality, since nothing of any real importance ever really happens."

"Define importance," the lighter alien countered.

"Define define!" the darker alien said.

The lighter alien addressed Vossoff and Nimmitz. "See? The nihilistic viewpoint belongs to whoever's the chair at the moment. We switch opinions when we switch positions. That way we both get to experience all possible points of view."

"Except phenomenology," said the darker alien. "I hate that."

"No," the lighter alien said, "you only imagine you hate

that."

Nimmitz grabbed Vossoff plaintively. "Get me away from this planet, Ernst. I don't like this place."

"In a minute," Vossoff sympathized. He turned his attention back to the two aliens. "I need to know this: How do you handle the basic necessities of life here?"

The lighter alien looked offended. "Philosophy is a basic necessity of life."

"I mean, how can you survive when there's no food here?"

"Ahhhh, that's the highest achievement of our advanced civilization. As we grew increasingly advanced, we also grew increasingly aware that the true mark of advancement was an uncluttered lifestyle. So one day we left our previous highly advanced civilization, used our all-powerful technology to create this planet, and imbued it with all manner of trans-dimensional mechanisms for supporting our existence here, including the translation program you've already encountered, a field that nourishes life without benefit of food, and — most importantly, given our rigorous aesthetic principles — an accommodation for preserving the physical status quo, which includes among other things regularly purging the landscape of all the annoying superfluous detail that accrues over time."

"Like chairs," the darker alien said. "Or starships."

"Or visitors," said the lighter alien.

"Yes," the darker alien said. "That, too, would be an excellent example."

There was a moment of uncannily uncomfortable silence.

Then the two humans yelped and began to run.

"I thought they'd never leave," said the lighter alien.

"Define never," said his companion the chair.

Vossoff and Nimmitz got back to their ship before the planet purged it from the landscape, but they didn't stop hyperventilating until they were safely back in orbit.

"That was close," gasped Nimmitz.

"Yes, it certainly was."

"Are we gonna leave this system now?"

Vossoff chuckled. "Absolutely not, my friend. This planet is a major business opportunity."

Nimmitz stared at him. "I don't get it."

"Weren't you listening at all? A field that nourishes life without recourse to food? Do you know what that would be worth on the open market? Hell, the food service industries alone would pay us several fortunes just to forget what we know!"

"But — that thing which gets rid of starships!"

"The most lucrative weapons system ever devised? What of it? Besides, we're safe. If the mechanism in question is still functional — the safest possible thing to assume, as I freely admit — then that must be because it monitors the planet only intermittently. We were lucky enough to land and take off during its dormant cycle, and we'll continue to be lucky as long we just take the time to determine the length of that cycle."

"I don't know," Nimmitz said. "I don't want to hang around any planet where people sit on each other like that."

But Vossoff was the one who won all their arguments, and so they dropped five probes into the desert, spaced 100 clicks apart. The probes were jet-black and perfectly spherical and they sat on the endless white plain like aloof things that refused to mix. The near-nothingness was almost worse than the absolute nothingness that had been there before; it made both Vossoff and Nimmitz yearn for something epic and brilliant to connect the dots. But there wasn't. Just a planet-sized blank piece of paper, as if God

Himself had woken up with writer's block.

And, as Nimmitz considerately kept pointing out, a couple of aliens, taking turns being the chair.

The probes sat on the white desert for thirty-two hours.

And then they disappeared.

No slow fading away, no dramatic lightshow, no eerie whining noise as the alien cleaning mechanism warmed up — just the five black probes, first there, then not.

Not satisfied at all, Vossoff dropped another five probes into the desert. They each sat in place for sixty-five hours, then disappeared, between one second and the next. He dropped one more. It disappeared in sixty-five hours. Another one. It disappeared in sixty-five hours. One more. Sixty-five hours.

"I think that's clear enough," Vossoff said.

"Yeah," Nimmitz said. "But I still can't believe they sit on each other like that."

"Is that a weapon?"

From any other advanced sentient it would have been an incredibly stupid question. The blaster was the length of Vossoff's arm and ended in a wicked-looking emission lens that had already partially melted from the backlash of the last six occasions Vossoff had been forced to use it. Neither Vossoff or Nimmitz really believed they needed the heavy artillery to capture one of the sentients, but they both knew the value of good public relations.

"Yes," Vossoff said. "It is a weapon."

"How fascinating," said the lighter alien. "It has been a long time since either one of us saw a weapon, the entire concept of weaponry being so inherently uncivilized and all."

"You're right about that," Vossoff said, in the gravelly

tone of a dangerous man who clearly wanted to be recognized as dangerous. "We are extremely uncivilized. We are morally and ethically in the same league as the barbarians who sacked Rome, and the cads who burned the Great Library of Alexandria, and the Centaurii raiders who installed stereo speakers on the Silent Colossus of Parnajan. We have no respect for your ancient advanced civilization, entertain nothing but contempt for your grand and glorious traditions, and wouldn't suffer any guilt about expunging your entire — admittedly, only two person — population. Therefore, we strongly urge you, as you value your lives, to come with us."

"Why should we do that? You sound like perfectly horrid people."

"Because," Vossoff explained, with perhaps a little more patience than the situation warranted, "being perfectly horrid people, if you don't come with us, we will cruelly and barbarically reduce the two of you to ash."

"The question," pointed out the darker alien, "is how we can intelligently regard ash as a lesser state of being when we who have personally not experienced that transformation have no intelligent basis for comparison. After all, for all we know, ash might be a step up. We need hard data."

"I was ash once," said the lighter alien. "I didn't like it much, but everybody has the right to enjoy their own chosen lifestyle."

Fed up, Vossoff blasted the darker alien out of existence. The lighter alien seemed to hover in the air a split second before falling to the ground. He did not look particularly upset, or even surprised, as he ran his fingers over the smooth featureless ground.

"Ernst!" Nimmitz shouted. "You shot the guy!"

"Grow up," snarled Vossoff. He turned his attention back to the one surviving alien. "Any questions?"

The alien was still running his fingers over the ground. "Yes," he said. "Where's the ash?"

"There's no ash. The disintegration is too thorough. The ash was just a convenient hyperbole I used to help you visualize your own destruction."

"Ahhh. We used to have hyperboles, too, but we eventually rejected them as uncivilized. — Unfortunately, it still leaves me without a chair. Which of you two gentlemen is going to volunteer?"

Nimmitz stepped back. "I ain't going to be a chair for nobody!"

Vossoff addressed the alien with the exaggerated care of any man speaking to a highly civilized idiot. "You miss the point. I am taking you prisoner. You are coming to my starship and you are going to tell me all the secrets of your advanced technology, because if you don't, I'm going to shoot you next."

"Then nobody will have a chair."

"Which will be wonderfully convenient, since there won't be anybody left on the planet to need a chair."

"Well, there is that," the alien conceded.

"You're getting on my nerves. I'm going to count to ten and then give you the same treatment I gave your friend. One. Two. Three . . ."

"There are chairs back on the ship!" Nimmitz cried.

It was the first time Nimmitz had opened his mouth during the negotiations, and the first time the alien seemed at all impressed by anything. "Soft chairs?"

"Sure!" Nimmitz said.

"The kind which lean back, so I can put my feet up?"

"Absolutely."

"And vibrating cushions, to gently ease away all my stress and tension like an entirely new adventure in comfort and bliss?"

"Hey," Nimmitz said expansively, "would I lie to you?"

"Well, then, why didn't you say so in the first place? It shall be a honor and privilege being taken prisoner by you." And with that, the alien stood up and sided with Nimmitz.

Vossoff put his hand over his eyes.

Nimmitz gave him a pitying look. "That's your problem, Ernst. You just got to know how to talk to people."

They'd been interrogating the alien aboard their ship for almost three days. He didn't mind, since he just loved lounging in Nimmitz's favorite recliner, basking in the heat of a ultra-violet lamp while sipping a tall glass of Vossoff's favorite scotch through a straw. "This is what I call a chair. Have I said that yet? Well, never mind. The eternal verities bear repeating. This is what I call a chair. It's highly decadent, and it hugs the back in a downright uncivilized way, but definitely, this . . . is . . . what I call a chair."

He'd made that speech, or some reasonably close variant, an average of once an hour since coming on board.

"I'm going to kill him," muttered Nimmitz.

"Just give me another hour. I promise you I'll make some progress." Vossoff turned his attention toward the alien. "You hear what's going on? My partner wants to shoot you. I'm the only thing holding him back. If you're smart, you'll cooperate."

"I know this routine," the alien said. "Good Sentient, Bad Sentient, right? Excellent for interrogation. My people used the technique, too, before we got civilized."

"Try to pay attention to me, please. Last night, we established that your extra-dimensional nourishment thingie operates on another plane of existence?"

"Yes. The mechanism — excuse me while I fluff these cushions — is run by the same highly advanced management protocol that keeps the amount of surface detail on the planetary surface an absolute constant. This is highly convenient, though it is of course hard on material things like chairs."

"And living organisms?"

"Oh, certainly. Were there any more than two creatures on the planet during any one of its periodic sweeps, the mechanism would eliminate them as superfluous detail."

Vossoff and Nimmitz looked at each other. The secrets of life and death, all wrapped up in a flaky little biped who liked to sip scotch through a straw. "Can we access this mechanism?" Vossoff asked.

"Why would you want to do a silly thing like that?"

"Because I have the weapon," Vossoff said.

The alien paused to consider that. "Very well. — I have lost track of time. How long before the next cycle?"

Vossoff checked his chronometer. "Ten of our hours."

"Then," said the alien, "I will help you access the mechanism in ten hours."

It was two minutes before the purification cycle, and Nimmitz was growing increasingly nervous.

"Listen, Ernst. I say we drop him off on the planet, take off, and get the hell out of this system as fast as we can."

Vossoff emitted laughter. "You've never been a smart man, but I never thought you were a coward. The profit —"

"Profit, shmofit. This whole deal stinks of Things Man Was Not Meant to Know."

"You're that scared of a little risk?"

"This isn't a little risk. Little risks are golden idols. Illicit drugs. Old comic books. Not highly advanced technology from an Ancient Civilization Far More Advanced Than Man. We could end up getting blasted to ash."

"Well," Vossoff said, merrily enough, "never having been ash, we don't have a basis for comparison. It might be a step up."

"Ernst —"

"I don't want to hear it!" Vossoff snapped, in the same dangerous tone he'd used when threatening the two lazy-butt aliens. "You want to be a small-timer forever, that's your business! But I've waited all my life for a score like this, and I'm not letting you blow it!"

"Excuse me," the alien said.

They both whirled at the sound of his voice. He'd been napping in the command chair, which he'd already said was even more comfortable than Nimmitz's lounger; by far, he said, the most spectacular decadent seating arrangement he'd encountered in his many millennia of existence. For a being from an Ancient and Highly Advanced Civilization that had evolved past the need for chairs, he really did seem to have a one-track-mind on the subject. It had been a relief to take a break from his interrogation, so they didn't have to listen to him. Vossoff said, "Yes?"

"The cleaning cycle starts in forty of your seconds," said the alien. "The interface has informed me it's available for reprogramming."

Vossoff all but leaped to the alien's side. "All right! — Tell it you want command controls!"

"Very well," said the alien. "How do you want it reprogrammed?"

"We want direct access to the nutritional mechanism. And the life-support mechanism. And the planetary purification device."

The alien did a double take. "Oh, is that all?"

"What do you mean, is that all?"

"I thought you were going to ask me something hard."

"We are. We want to profit from the secrets of your ancient and highly advanced civilization."

"But you don't need me for that," the alien said. "You're going to start benefiting from them in twenty seconds."

"What do you mean?"

The surface of the planet started pulsating in waves.

"It's searching for us," said the alien.

"What?"

"My companion and I. Remember, it's supposed to keep the degree of surface detail constant. That means replacing anything that gets removed. Without us, it's going to have to come up with the nearest equivalent substitute."

"Sub —"

"Two sentients," The alien said. "Same species."

Vossoff and Nimmitz looked at each other.

"I really do envy you," said the alien sadly. "Enjoying the benefits of such an ancient and advanced civilization. Me, I'm just going to have to make do, opening a furniture store somewhere . . ."

When the light faded, they were standing on the planet's surface, facing each other from five yards apart.

Nimmitz spoke first: "I ain't gonna be the chair."

Just a Couple of Extinct Aliens Riding Around in a Limo

Looking for employment in extraterrestrial want ads is always risky. Nine times out of ten, they're seeking organ donors for their finer restaurants.

But looking for employment in extraterrestrial want ads, when you're a pair of notorious criminals hunted in half the civilized universe, despised laughingstocks in the other half, and so low on cash that you debase yourself by collecting the sentient deposit bottles that run wild on the littered streets of P'psi VII, is so clearly an invitation to disaster that even Vossoff and Nimmitz should have known better. However, they were desperate; their last scheme, a failed attempt to loot the fabled advanced civilization of Fyliss IV (where they'd still be stranded if they hadn't been lucky enough to hitch a ride on a robotic interplanetary bookmobile), had cost the pair their starship, their pride in their reputations, and everything they'd ever managed to steal; and they'd been eking out a meager existence on P'psi's mean streets ever since.

It was Vossoff who discovered a possible way out late

one night, while scrolling through a stolen copy of the local newspad in search of the few jobs a human being could hold without the amputation or grafting-on of limbs. He woke Nimmitz. "Hey."

Nimmitz, who'd been deep in a nightmare about aliens who talk about nothing but easy chairs, woke groggily. "What."

"You and I are about to become parents."

Nimmitz sat up at once, his normally tiny eyes bulging with revulsion and terror. "Jeez, Ernst, I swear to God I didn't know that was the way it worked on this planet!"

"Keep your mind out of the gutter, swine. I'm referring to the want ads. Check out this beauty: *NEED OBSCENELY VAST AMOUNTS OF CASH IN A HURRY? ADOPT AN EXTINCT ALIEN. Many species available, no actual work involved. We pay for all filing costs, transportation, future expenses, plus a habitable planet engineered to your specifications, and a ten-billion credit honorarium. No time travel involved; references not required. Contact Miss Melinda Haversham, Charles Darwin Clearinghouse for Extinct Alien Species, care of* blahblahblahblah. Did you hear that, my oafish friend? Ten billion credits, a free planet engineered to our specifications, and no work required! This time tomorrow we'll be well on our way to riches!"

Nimmitz eyed the newspad warily. "I don't know, Ernst. It sounds too easy to me."

Vossoff sneered, thumbing the glowing spot on the screen to instantly print out a hard copy. "Adopting an extinct alien species? Why would you expect it to be hard?"

And, indeed, the actual mechanics of the adoption turned out to be not difficult at all. All Vossoff had to do was enter the nearest hytex, punch in the toll-free number in the ad, assure the AI receptionist that he had spent long days and nights wrestling with his conscience over the plight of all the —

— (here he went overboard sobbing) —

— poor, pathetic, extinct alien species out there. His conscience left him no choice, he said, but to accept ten billion credits and a free planet in their memory.

He wasn't off the hytex for ten seconds before a sleek hyperspace limo, three P'psian city blocks long, materialized at the curb, its wet bar and disgustingly servile crew waiting. Vossoff hopped in at once, Nimmitz only after searching the sky above for the falling anvil he expected the universe to arrange any minute soon.

The trip took a week. Vossoff spent most of it in a merry state of inebriation, flirting with the flight attendants and thoroughly enjoying himself despite Nimmitz' constant niggling about the (thus far) purely theoretical anvil.

At the end of the line, the limo deposited them on a lovely little planet of brilliant blue skies and rolling green meadows where an angelic little old lady wearing a pink shawl of real earth wool sat sweetly knitting on the porch of her adorable little red schoolhouse.

Nimmitz was paralyzed. "It's a trap. She's going to eat us."

"Nonsense," said Vossoff. "She doesn't have the proper jaw structure. Isn't it more reasonable to assume that she's actually going to do what the ad said, and pay us the equivalent of a planetary treasury, just for doing absolutely nothing?"

"Because she looks like my Aunt Rose," said Nimmitz, "and my Aunt Rose would eat us."

Which was true; Vossoff remembered reading something about it in the tabloids a few years back. He shook his head to clear his mind of the foul image. "Let me handle this. You don't know how to talk to people."

The angelic little old lady was, of course, Miss Melinda Haversham, founder and administrator of the Charles Darwin Clearinghouse for Extinct Alien Species . . . and she was so overjoyed to meet Vossoff and Nimmitz that the pair had to suffer through almost an hour of tedious small talk about orchids before she finally got down to the real reason for their meeting. "Yes," she said. "You read the ad correctly. Ten billion credits and ownership of a customized planet just for agreeing to adopt an Extinct Alien Species."

"That's insanely generous," noted Vossoff.

She asjusted her bifocals. "Well, we're a nonprofit organization. Being insanely generous is what we're all about."

"Do you mind me asking where all the money comes from?"

"Well, it is a rude question, but not one I particularly mind answering. We're a special public-service project of Bettelhine Munitions."

Nimmitz almost spilled his tea on the rug. "You can't mean the fiends responsible for the Ultimate Dreadnaught!"

"The very same," chuckled Miss Haversham.

Vossoff and Nimmitz met each other's eyes. Even they had been horrified by the capabilities of the Bettelhine Ultimate Dreadnaught . . . a warship the size of a small sun, that required the natural resources of a thousand planets just to build, bankrupted a hundred planetary treasuries just to finance, and was capable of routinely scooping up entire inhabited planets just to fire them like cannonballs. Rumor had it that the entire population of the evil warlike race that had commissioned it was still wandering about aimlessly inside, in fruitless search for the hidden control room that would enable them to conquer everybody.

"Mr. Bettelhine always felt guilty about that," Miss Haversham admitted. "Not about the Dreadnaught, of course, since it was after all never used, but for all the other fine Bettelhine Munitions products that have laid waste to so many planets across the galaxy, at reasonable prices that even the budget rampaging warmonger could afford. As partial atonement, he endowed the Clearinghouse . . . a place dedicated to the memory of all the intelligent alien races wiped out by his company. Here, compassionate sentients like yourselves can be paid handsomely for offering their last respects to the memory of all these noble races so violently expunged from the universe."

"It's certainly enough to bring a tear to my eye," agreed Vossoff. "When do we get paid handsomely?"

"Why, as soon as you decide which Extinct Alien Species to adopt." She passed Vossoff a book. "There are over one hundred needy candidates pictured in this catalogue. We have another ten thousand on file on in our library. You can, if you wish, stay here as our guests while researching the Extinct Alien Species that most fits your aesthetic standards . . ."

"Ernst . . ." said Nimmitz. "I don't like this place, Ernst."

Vossoff ignored him and examined the catalogue, which had a cover as gut-wrenchingly purple as the molten rock that the terrible cannibal leeches of Terrix V use to balm their throats during their frequent stomach upsets. When he opened the cover, he discovered that it was a Holographic Pop-Up Projector, with startlingly realistic 3-D representations of various Extinct Alien Species eagerly leaping from its pages like vaudeville performers desperate to catch a producer's eye. Within seconds, he spotted a four-legged creature with a pair of tiny heads waving at the end of long serpentine necks . . . a tusked humanoid with four arms . . . and a pulpy mass packed inside some kind of huge seed-pod. None of these specimens particularly struck him as great losses to the great galactic gene-pool, but he supposed that didn't matter. He wouldn't need to harbor genuine affection for any of them in order to claim the hefty award for an adoption. Still, rather than decide too quickly and possibly jeopardize the deal, he made a big show of pretending that he really cared which Extinct Alien Species he and Nimmitz chose . . .

Halfway through the catalogue, he found that it did matter. "Well, what do you know. This is interesting. Here, Nimmitz. Isn't this interesting?"

Nimmitz goggled. "It's disgusting, is what it is."

"Oh, no, I'm not referring to the Species itself . . . which," he added, to reassure Miss Haversham, "I must admit, truly looks like a noble and handsome race. No, I'm referring to the little red notation at the bottom of the page, which says that choosing this particular species doubles the stipend. Can that possibly be so?"

Miss Haversham took a look. "Ah, yes," she said, daintily wiping a tear from the corner of one eye. "That's the Pylthothi Screaming Stink-Moss. Truly, one of our most deserving cases. A moist, grayish-black creature, indigenous to the subterranean volcanic caves on Pylthothus III, it spent its ten-million-year lifespan clinging to stone walls, dripping acidic slime, emitting incessant bloodcurdling screams, and feeding off the vile sulphurous fumes that constantly belched forth from the planet's molten depths. When first discovered by a mining expedition, only two centuries ago, the Stink-Moss was thought to be just another foul-smelling Pylthothi plant, but further study revealed an intelligent, sensitive creature with a highly advanced social structure, that communicated with others of its kind via a highly sophisticated language primarily composed of toxic gaseous wastes. Alas, the entire population perished when the planet was blown up as an icebreaker during a Bettelhine Corporate Bonding Session of a few years ago . . ."

"Go figure," mourned Vossoff. "And they had everything to live for, too. — But despite the unlimited inherent fascination of your interminably long and unbearably heart-rending tale, which we certainly appreciate, you still haven't answered the question I actually asked. To rephrase: have you really doubled the standard compensation for adopting this particular extinct species?"

"Yes, sir, we have. We did that because the Pylthothi Screaming Stink-Moss is truly a hardship case. Most adoption applicants only have sympathy for Extinct Alien Species either close to their own genotype, like the wide selection of humanoids at our disposal, or cute Extinct Alien Species, like unicorns or time otters or balls of fur that purr mindlessly when stroked. The Pylthothi, on the other hand, were unique in the universe, had no sympathizers close to their genotype, and were almost pathologically uncute, being in fact so vile in every way that nobody wants to be associated with them, even in memory. Personally, I don't even like looking at that page."

"Neither do I," said Nimmitz. "Let's go, Ernst."

"Not yet," said Vossoff. He flipped the page, found an unbearably adorable pink lemur-thing with soulful eyes that could wrench tears from a stone, yawned with boredom, and turned his attention back to the Pylthothi. They were revolting, all right. And yet, that wonderful stipend . . .

. . . Vossoff sighed. He hated to admit it, but for once in his singly braincelled life, Nimmitz was right. There had to be a catch.

He said, "Let me get this straight. Twenty billion credits and a customized planet . . . just for adopting this species."

"Yes," said Miss Haversham.

"This *Extinct* Species."

"That is correct."

"This uncommonly awful, thoroughly unpleasant Species."

"Yes, sir."

"This species so completely expunged from the universe that this hologram is all that remains."

"Yes, sir."

"You're sure they're extinct, now."

"Yes, sir."

"You don't have any stray Pylthothi Screaming Stink-Moss sharing their charms with your back offices?"

"No, sir."

"There are no previously-undiscovered specimens that will be peeled off the wallpaper and dumped on our laps the second we sign the contract?"

"None, sir. There's no Pylthothi, anywhere."

"You're certain."

Miss Havisham's eyes were starting to glaze. "Yes, sir."

Vossoff hesitated. "Forgive me for harping on this, ma'am, but . . . well, my partner and I have been burned before. You're, ah, absolutely sure you're not going to surprise us with survivors you didn't know about until now, that my friend Nimmitz and I will then be contractually obligated to care for for the rest of our lives?"

"Yes, sir. We are unstinting in our research, and we know for a fact that there are now no more living or dead Pylthothi Screaming Stink-Moss remaining anywhere in the known universe. If you wish, I could provide you with a legal document absolving you and your friend Nimmitz of your end of the bargain if this turns out to be literally untrue."

"So you don't expect us to actually care for this flatulent fungus."

"No, sir. All you have to do is sign the papers certifying that you've officially adopted this extinct species, accept the check, and take a quick jaunt across the quadrant to sign for your customized planet. We do the rest."

"May I ask, then . . . what's the point?"

"Memory," sighed Miss Haversham. "There are just so many Extinct Alien Species out there . . . or rather, I should say, no longer out there. Too many for the universe to much note or long remember. But if we can pay people like you to adopt these species, even in those cases when you think the species in question are vile and disgusting, then we can keep the memory burning a little while longer. Or, to put it another way, gentlemen, by adopting this species, you are agreeing to be their monument. As for us, we get a tremendous tax break this way."

"And that's it," said Vossoff.

"That's it," agreed Miss Haversham.

Vossoff licked his lips, ran his hand over his great bald head, and turned to Vossoff. "Sounds pretty straightforward to me."

Nimmitz said, "Me too. I'm leaving."

Fortunately — or unfortunately, depending on just how deep your personal convictions about people getting what they deserve — Vossoff had always been the controlling stockholder in this particular partnership. They signed the papers. They adopted the Pylthothi species. They accepted a check for twenty billion credits. And after a sumptious home-cooked dinner (marred only by the strangely disagreeable aftertaste of the garlic bread), they boarded the space limo and departed in triumph, having started the day as a pair of has-been bums and ended it as two of the wealthiest men in the civilized galaxy.

Vossoff was so dazed by his easy victory, and Nimmitz

so obsessed with searching for that elusive plummeting anvil, that it was all of four hours before either one of them noticed a faint odor. Nimmitz went off to complain to the engineer; Vossoff simply ignored it and watched a spellbindingly bad in-flight movie made by some misguided alien producers who had thought they could duplicate an old-fashioned terran western using an all extraterrestrial cast. He thought the Aldebaranian squid-thing cast as Wyatt Earp (and wearing a standard-issue tin star and white hat) was worth the price of admission all by itself. Still, even that palled after a while, and before long Vossoff dozed off and enjoyed his favorite dream, in which he dove headfirst into a vast ocean of glittering cold coins. He'd been having this dream for years now . . . often at times of extreme poverty, when possessing even one of those coins would have seemed an improvement . . . and the dream had always betrayed him by having all that beautiful money taken away from him at the last minute, usually (for reasons that would always escape him) by a strangely-muttonchopped alien duck. Tonight, however, the dream ended differently. Tonight, the ocean of money melted in his hands, and the tropical skies darkened, and the world around him turned into a dark and forbidding underground chamber, billowing with thick clouds of bad-smelling alien gas.

Then he woke up and discovered that it was not entirely a dream. The odor was getting worse.

He was actually elated, because this gave him an opportunity to complain himself. And not with the humiliating hesitant politeness of a man with modest savings, but with the thundering, arrogant, unreasonable tantrum of a man with vast quantities of money. He could be as insulting and obnoxious as he wanted, ripping their fragile egos to bloody shreds, without even a scintilla of fear that anybody would jettison him from the airlock in retribution, as had always happened when he acted that way before. No, he was going to be a monster, and they were going to bow and scrape and take it. That, as he'd always understood it, was what being obscenely rich was all about.

He slipped on a robe and strode from his quarters, into the main lounge, where he found an exhausted Nimmitz sitting at the passenger terminal, scrolling through shipboard reference files.

"What's wrong with you?" Vossoff raged. "Don't you smell anything wrong with the air?"

Nimmitz didn't turn from the screen. "I complained again half an hour ago. The engineer assures me there's nothing wrong."

"And you accepted that? Is this ship really supposed to reek like a voshnoi stable?"

Nimmitz shrugged. "He said it's just the way it smells in here, that's all. I made him promise to take another look at the air purifiers anyway."

"He'd better if he wants to keep his job!" Vossoff snarled weakly, his enthusiasm already fading. Nimmitz was just no fun being irate at, that's all; the man had no talent for it. After a moment, more to break the silence than anything else, Vossoff said, "So what are you reading, anyway?"

"Encyclopedia article. All about the Pylthothi Screaming Stink-Moss."

It took Vossoff a second to recognize the phrase. "For Quarn's sake, why?"

Nimmitz averted his eyes. "Because we adopted the species. I figured it's . . . like . . . our responsibility, or something."

"You're out of your mind. If some wacked-out munitions magnate decides to salve his troubled conscience by handing out free fortunes, I don't particularly feel the need to make it a high school research project."

"Maybe not," said Nimmitz, "but do you know the real reason the Pylthothi screamed incessantly?"

"Is this a new kind of ethnic joke? Very well. What was the real reason the Pylthothi screamed incessantly?"

"According to this article, it's because . . . well, let me read this part out loud. *'While they were totally alien physically, the Pylthothi possessed an inborn aesthetic standard almost identical to humanity's. They were nauseated by the way they looked, sickened by the way they smelled, and utterly horrified by the way they lived. Most of all, they were tormented by the ten-million-year lifespan they had to suffer through it. To put it succinctly . . . they screamed incessantly because it was, under the circumstances, the way any reasonable creature would act.'*" Nimmitz looked away the screen. "Have I mentioned recently that I don't like this deal, Ernst?"

"It depends on your definition of recently. As I recall, you've been mentioning it just about hourly."

"I don't like this deal, Ernst."

"You don't like being handed a check for more money than the average annual income of some entire planetary civilizations?"

"Not until I know the catch," said Nimmitz.

"Why must there be a catch, all the time? Why can't you just believe that it's a genuine charity?"

"Two reasons," said Nimmitz. "One, I've never seen any."

Vossoff blinked. "And Two?"

"That smell you were complaining about?"

"Yes?"

"That really bad, acidic smell?"

"Yes?"

"The one that you're probably not sure you can stand?"

"Yes?"

"I think it's coming from us."
Vossoff started yelling.

They spent the next half hour frantically ransacking Vossoff's cabin for the P'psian newspad, retrieving it, and searching the Classifieds for the advertisement bearing the number of the Charles Darwin Clearinghouse. They spent the half-hour after that patching a call through the ship hytex, and the half-hour after that suffering through an interminable muzak rendition of a slapstick Betelgeusian operetta called "When Suns Go Pfffffft."

By the time Miss Haversham came on-screen, somehow no longer sweet and matronly, but instead cold and predatorial, her old-lady clothing now replaced by the harsh tailoring of a corporate shark, Vossoff was too livid to care. "You're in a whole lot of trouble, lady!"

"I find that hard to believe," said Miss Haversham.

"You never told us you were going to mess with our chromosomes, damn it!"

"Yes I did," Miss Haversham said coolly. "In fact, I was scrupulously careful with my language throughout the negotiation. I never said you were adopting the Pylthothi. I said that were you were adopting the Pylthothi species, which is something entirely different, and which, by any literal definition, means adopting the Pylthothi genetic structure as your own. It means adopting their appearance, their smell, their natural habitat, and their way of life. It means becoming a Pylthothi. Why else did you think we were paying you so much money?"

Nimmitz clutched Vossoff's arm. "What does she mean, Ernst? Please tell me what she means."

Vossoff tried to tell him, but no words emerged.

"No need to bother," Miss Haversham said kindly. "I'll tell him myself." She addressed Nimmitz. "You know that meal you ate before departing the Clearinghouse? Specifically, the strangely disagreeable aftertaste of the garlic bread? You were both rude enough to mention it. Well, that taste was the combined chemical exhaust of literally billions of nanorobotic microsurgeons, who entered your system through the aforementioned bread and have been busily revising your genetic structure one cell at a time ever since. By now, neither one of you is still quite human; by the time you reach your new world, in about forty-two hours, you'll both be Pylthothi enough to be transplanted there. Our representatives have selected a wonderful little cave wall where I'm sure you'll both spend the next ten million years being very happy."

Nimmitz blinked several times in rapid succession. "But I don't *want* to be a Pylthothi screaming stink-moss."

All Vossoff heard was the unmistakeable sound of Nimmitz's very, very large anvil plummeting toward him from somewhere in the vicinity of the Charles Darwin Clearinghouse.

"The check is good," said Miss Haversham. "If you'd just searched a little more carefully through our catalogues, like most of our clients, you might even have found yourselves a relatively humanoid species capable of cashing it. Poor planning, I think. But aside from that, gentlemen . . . our business is done."

Vossoff found voice. "But wait — !"

She broke the connection.

Nimmitz pouted. "But I don't *want* to be a Pylthothi screaming stink-moss."

Vossoff merely fainted.

It's not the stench that gets to them. Or the tedium of being rooted to a cave wall, unable to move. Or the frequent ground-quakes that once every hour or so tears through their little home like the death-throes of a dying beast. Or the constant maddening drip-drip-drip of their acidic secretions wearing away at the rocks below. Or even the knowledge that it was their own carelessness around the finer points of contract law that got them here. No; they scream because there's a clear permaplastic acid-proof display case on the cave floor between them. One designed to last for eons, that has been considerately left in their presence so they can see it.

It's their check.

Just a Couple of Space Rogues Playing Name That Tune

It took less than twenty minutes for their ship's medical diagnostic program to confirm that neither Vossoff and Nimmitz had suffered more than their usual amount of serious brain damage recently; they weren't seeing things; the solar system up ahead really was under attack by a giant pink bunny.

It wouldn't be precisely accurate to declare this the very last thing they'd ever expected to encounter, since the sight appeared nowhere on their list of expectations, not even in last place. And yet, there one was, nibbling at one small uninhabited planet it held between its paws, and reducing another to superheated plasma with disintegration beams fired from its twitching pink nose.

Vossoff did a more thorough scan and found out that the planet-devouring bunny was in fact an alien warship, built in this shape for reasons that both men assumed must have made some kind of sense to somebody at the time. Moreover, this particular solar system possessed a wealthy civilized world, Glorvia IV, which was frantically broadcasting distress signals on every known band as the remarkably cute dreadnaught continued to nibble everything in its path. Ship's Brain projections of the warship's progress revealed that without help Glorvia would be rabbit chow in just under six hours.

Vossoff twirled the tip of his walrus moustache as he watched the destruction unfold. "Interesting, wouldn't you say, eh, Karl? Just when you think the universe is getting dull, it exerts itself and restores your faith in its infinite variety."

Nimmitz was less thrilled. "I used to have a pet bunny rabbit, Ernst. Back when I was five. I don't like having my memories sullied this way."

"Hmmm. You never struck me as a man who would hold sacred his cherished memories of a childhood bunny rabbit. What was its name? Rascal, maybe? Or Bugs?"

"No, actually, it was . . ."

"I'm not really interested, Karl."

"But it was a really cute name. We called him . . ."

Vossoff clapped a hand over his partner's mouth. "Listen to me," he said, very slowly and very dangerously. "If you persist in telling me the name you called your bunny rabbit when you were five, you will spend the five seconds immediately following that unsolicited revelation hurtling from the airlock in an advanced case of explosive decompression. I didn't really want to know; I only expressed interest to mock you." He removed his hand. "Do you understand?"

Nimmitz pouted. "But you asked . . ."

Vossoff almost dove for the silverware. He demurred only because he recognized that both he and Nimmitz had been under an unusual amount of stress lately; they'd only recently escaped from a remote planet where they'd spent a full decade trapped in a cave after being genetically transformed into a spectacularly unpleasant form of sentient alien moss. They'd be there still, courtesy of the powerful munitions company that had tricked them into agreeing to the change, had an independent government auditor inspecting the books not discovered that Nimmitz had accidentally mis-spelled his own name, rendering both his signature, and the contract, void.

Recovery came slowly after something like that, even with the aid of well-paid geneticists; for instance, Vossoff still secreted acid at unpredictable moments, frequently enough to sear away his clothes with no warning, and render him a surprise hit at cocktail parties. Still, a business opportunity like this might be just the ticket to get back on track again. And so he addressed the Brain: "Send a message to the Glorvians. Tell them we'll be happy to drive off the bunny, in exchange for a mere ninety percent of their collected wealth. Make sure you specify that this does not include expenses, which may run as high as the remaining ten percent. Backed up against the wall the way they are, I'm sure they'll agree to our generous terms with no problems."

"Yo," said the Ship's Brain.

Nimmitz blinked. "Do you really think we oughta get involved with this, Ernst? We're not set up for great cosmic battles right now. We don't even have long-range blasters on this rig."

"Maybe not," shrugged Vossoff, "but it's always rabbit season, somewhere..."

The instant the Glorvians eagerly accepted his terms, Vossoff got on the hytex and broadcast a universal white-flag signal to the giant bunny.

Nimmitz's huge brow knit with a determined lack of comprehension that not even nuclear weaponry could have dented. "I don't like this, Ernst. That's an awfully big bunny."

"Obviously," said Vossoff. "That's the key to the whole puzzle."

"Huh?"

"Someday, I'm going to have to take you to a public genomat and treat you to your first IQ point. — Don't you see how hard it must have been engineering that dreadnought to look and move like a Terran bunny? Designing robotics to drive the legs, installing motors to keep the pink nose twitching, wrapping the whole thing in a fuzzy metallic coat capable of looking soft and fluffy under interstellar conditions, and arming it with what must be tremendously advanced quantum dampers to keep it from being torn to pieces by the tidal forces of the planets it catches between its paws? Especially when you consider that if these are the kind of folks who go around destroying whole solar systems at a clip, then they're probably also the kind of folks who don't like bunny rabbits in the first place?"

"Not like bunny rabbits?" gasped Nimmitz. "The fiends!"

"The real question," Vossoff said doggedly, "is why they went to all that trouble, when the average genocidal warmonger wouldn't bother. Which is why it's so important to establish a dialogue. Once we determine their reasoning, we'll be well on our way to knowing how to —"

The Ship's Brain broke in. "Yo. Boss. The alien warship just sent a return message."

"Holo?"

"Nope. Audio only."

It was better than nothing. Vossoff said, "Play it."

What followed was the most ungodly yelling either Vossoff or Nimmitz had heard in years. It sounded a little like cats turned inside-out by matter transmission, and a lot like the new hit album by the Exploding Idiots, except in both cases considerably less musical.

It went on like that for a while. It didn't get any better.

Nimmitz rubbed his bald scalp with the dedication of a man struggling to confirm that his skull was still intact underneath. "My head hurts."

Vossoff chuckled. "I find this fascinating, myself. An entirely tonal language. Reminds me of the Orbisonians of Wilbrii IX, who have to hold a single high note for years at a time just to say hello. — Brain, can you translate any of that?"

"That is translated," said the Brain.

There was a moment of uncomfortable, not even remotely blessed, silence, as both Vossoff and Nimmitz struggled to accept that as a reasonable answer.

Vossoff leaned closer to the screen. "Come again?"

"You heard me right, boss. The giant bunny's entire transmission consists of incoherent yelling."

Nimmitz said, "Reminds me of us, the way we usually end up." When Vossoff glared at him, he stuck out his lower lip petulantly: "Well, it does."

"There are certain surface similarities," conceded the Brain. "But I've also run a complete tonal analysis, searching for the stress indicators common to most sentient species, and I can detect no overt signs of your usual terror or despair. In fact, I think it's baby talk."

Vossoff drummed his fingertips on the control panel, ruminating that thought, as if it were some cosmic cud and he the great galactic cow. As he concentrated, his thick, bushy eyebrows knit together so tightly they looked like they were mating. Eventually, he brightened. "Brain?"

"Yo."

"Please send that vessel another message. In baby talk. No content whatsoever. Sweeten it so it's the right tone and pitch, loop it and play it loud on all available channels."

"Yo," said the Brain, as it signed off.

Nimmitz frowned at the view screen — where the

giant fluffy bunny was even now adorably twitching its powder puff tail — and then at Vossoff, who was contemplating a bottle of the ship's finest champagne. He scratched his head, started to say something, found something on the ceiling compelling enough to stare at, then, at long last, admitted his secret shame: "I don't get it, Ernst."

Vossoff chugged directly from the bottle. "Gee, that's a shocker."

The giant bunny on the view screen abruptly paused mid-meal, faced them with the closest thing any bunny can get to fascination. As they watched, one of its moist brown eyes slid open, revealing a vast, shiny docking bay easily large enough to accommodate their own tiny spaceship with room to spare. The landing lights were on and blinking.

"You know," said Vossoff, "sometimes I'm so brilliant I even astound myself."

Nimmitz merely scratched his head worriedly.

The interior of the alien dreadnaught turned out to be hospitable to human life in all the important ways, and thoroughly irritating in all the unimportant ones.

The important ways included the breathable atmosphere, the comfortable ambient temperature, and the apparently total absence of things like squadrons of implacable indestructible hunter-killer robots bristling with high-tech weaponry and programmed to ruthlessly exterminate all intruders.

These were good things.

The unimportant ways mostly consisted of the deafening ungodly racket. The endless incoherent screaming that echoed loudly from elsewhere in the ship was not nearly as annoying as the even louder Muzak, that resembled a melody about as much as the North America nebula, seen from inside, actually resembled a continent. The melody was bright and cheery and filled with zest for life and it was therefore instantly depressing beyond belief.

As they emerged from their ship and took their first clumsy steps onto the oddly padded floors of the docking bay, Nimmitz said, "Ernst? I think I recognize the tune."

"I'm thoroughly impressed that you can even discern one. The composer should be flogged."

"No, really. I used to listen to this every afternoon when I was a kid. It was the theme music of the X'norr'gthi the Carnosaur show. Remember?"

"Oh, Lord, no." Vossoff moaned, because now that Nimmitz mentioned it, he did remember. A creation of the evil Nahnseekai Empire, who were at that time at war with everybody, X'norr'gthi the Carnosaur had been an insidious propaganda show shown on most holo systems and virtual reality networks throughout the known universe. Essentially just another jolly striped foam-rubber lizard, he'd captured the imaginations of an entire generation by teaching life-affirming lessons like "You Will All Be Destroyed." Billions of children all over the galaxy had defected to the enemy, only to return in hordes when they turned old enough to find X'norr'gthi as thoroughly insipid as their parents did.

"Great galaxies," Nimmitz said sentimentally, "I missed this stuff."

"You would," muttered Vossoff. "But I'm glad you identified it for me. It leads me to believe my theory is correct. Come on." He led Nimmitz to the huge double-doors at the far end of the docking bay, which opened automatically as the two men approached. "This should take us to the control room. In the meantime, I suppose I owe you an explanation, so listen carefully: imagine you belong to the ruling class of a ruthless warmongering alien race."

Nimmitz stood stock-still and closed his eyes. "Okay."

Vossoff entered the elevator — which itself was large enough to admit a five-story building — then realized Nimmitz hadn't joined him and yanked him aboard. "What are you doing?"

"I'm imagining."

"Can't you imagine and follow me at the same time?"

"Not vividly," said Nimmitz.

"Imagine less-than-vividly and keep up with me."

"Okay," said Nimmitz, imagining less than vividly.

The huge elevator automatically closed, and began to descend. Vossoff incinerated the stereo speakers with his pocket blaster, just to silence the bouncy idiocies of the X'norr'ghti theme song, and spoke quickly: "All right. You belong to the ruling class of a ruthless warmongering alien race. You can't be home with your children all the time because you're usually away in other solar systems, conquering people. Who do you get to baby-sit the kids?"

Nimmitz blinked. "I don't know. Depends if the next-door neighbors have a teenaged daughter who needs mad money."

"Nice try, but she's probably in your gunnery hatch, nuking the orphanages and hospitals. No . . . if you're truly demented enough, you commission Baby's First Warship, automate it enough to be piloted by a gurgling infant, install the little tyke as captain, and let the kid run amuck in solar systems where nobody has sufficient firepower to fight back. That way, when you're back from cutting your bloody swath through the universe, you can pick up the kid, and coo indulgently over all the emerging civilizations it wiped out during your absence. Got that?"

About thirty seconds later, Nimmitz did. "Wait a m-inute. You're telling me that's why it's shaped like a giant bunny?"

"Precisely."

"That's crazy!"

"I agree. Unfortunately, it's not my fault some parents dress their kids funny."

"B-but . . . how would the baby even know it was *in* a giant bunny?"

"I posit some sort of advanced virtual reality technology, hooked up to the baby's visual cortex, but frankly, it doesn't really matter whether the baby knows or not. Toys intended for infants don't have to be sold to the infant, but to its parents, who thanks to inescapable psychological associations will invariably want something representationally cute. Like a terrestrial bunny, which just happens to be a primary symbol of cuteness throughout the cosmos."

"Even if the bunny's destroying inhabited planets?"

"Especially if the bunny's destroying inhabited planets! Warlike races are like that! Have you ever heard of the Jannai, for instance? They bombarded innocent worlds with enzymatic cannons capable of reducing animal life to liquid protoplasm, until the entire planetary surface was covered with warm icky goo. Why? Because their kids liked finger-painting. Next to that, this is downright cuddly."

"And why did it let us inside?"

"Because when I sent that return message in baby talk, the ship's translation program invited me inside to play." Vossoff cracked his knuckles proudly. "All very elementary stuff, really."

"Yeah," said Nimmitz. "Like wanting to run and hide."

After that, the elevator descended several kilometers in silence, the only sounds being Vossoff chortling in anticipation of his imminent riches, and Nimmitz moaning as he waited to be bitten by the familiar iron jaws of fate.

They were deep in the belly of the bunny, two hours later, when the elevator came to a stop, and the light over the immense elevator doors helpfully went ding.

The doors slid open, revealing —

Well, let's put it this way.

There exists a great deal of rude barroom debate, among the rummies of the cosmos, over which intelligent species bears the ugliest young. The top contenders of this honor include the K'cenhowten, whose offspring resemble mangos thrown into propeller blades, the SheeTetas, whose little lumps of joy are frequently mistaken for free-ranging goiters, and the Pylthothi, about whom the less said the better. But even they wouldn't have placed so highly had they been forced to compete with this creature.

Not that its appearance was even remotely alien. Far from it: its phenotype was as close to humanoid as a fifty-meter baby subject to all the limitations of the square-cube law could possibly be. But it was also possessed of the power-hungry scowl common only to those species vile enough to be Machiavellian at birth — a face a mother could have loved only if that mother were one of the Borgias. Fortunately for Vossoff and Nimmitz, it didn't immediately notice it had visitors, as all its attention was occupied by the floating holographic bunny busily eating a holographic planet at eye-level. As the two men watched, the baby tilted its head slightly, directing the holographic bunny to take another chomp of the unfortunate holographic planet; when the western hemisphere split in two, the baby expressed its approval with an enthusiastic, "*Aaaaaaaaaaahhhhhhhhhhhh!*"

The chamber was filled with life-support machinery for the tremendous tot — including roaring aqueducts that provided tsunami of strained fruit for its feeding, gigantic steaming vats dedicated to sterilizing its tent-sized diapers, and dozens of humanoid metallic servitors who fluttered about dabbing its delicate skin with tons of soft white powder.

Nimmitz took one look at the baby and almost toppled from vertigo. "Gee, I hope for the mother's sake the birth was Caesarean."

Vossoff resisted sincerely thanking Nimmitz for the wonderful image. "Hey, see that cube-shaped machine over there?"

"The one shaped like a cube?"

"Yes, Karl, the one shaped like a cube. I'm sorry if I wasn't specific enough for you."

"That's okay," said Nimmitz. "I see it."

"Well, that's a Bettelhine Munitions Mark VIII Navigational Databank. It's loaded with complete files on all the planetary systems in the known universe. Ten to one, this one's been programmed with specially customized subroutines subtly steering the tot to the places where his doting parents would like him to run amuck. So it shouldn't take me more than five minutes to hack the program, change the parameters, and steer the kid away from this solar system. We'll have saved an entire civilization — and become very, very rich men — without even breaking a sweat."

"And what's that structure over there?" Nimmitz pointed. "The great big spherical thing, with the rod sticking out of it?"

Vossoff peered at the distant spherical thing, and frowned. He didn't know. It was set on the ground, right beside the pilot. He doubted that it had anything to do with navigation, which was the most immediate problem, but it resembled no other space-travel paraphernalia he'd ever seen, which meant that it could conceivably be some kind of cutting-edge technology unknown to Man. The idea of stealing its design, and thus making not one but two immense fortunes in one day, was too outrageous to exist. "Tell you what," he said. "I deal with the Databank, you investigate that sphere. Find out what you can about it, without touching anything, and I'll meet you there in a few minutes to tell you why you got it all wrong."

"Sure," said Nimmitz. He turned to go, walked five steps, and committed a perfect indignant double take. "Hey!"

Reprogramming the Databank didn't take Vossoff five minutes. It took six. But that was only because the wiring was crusted over with strained vegetables — apparently Junior liked to throw his food, and the edible paste had dripped down the bulkhead and gotten into the machinery. It wasn't an insurmountable problem; after all, Nimmitz, who had similar table manners, frequently splattered their own hyperdrive generator the same way.

Vossoff deftly cobbled up a new program which would encourage the pilot toward an uninhabited system some fifty light years away, and stopped just short of activating it, before using his pocket hytex to contact the imperiled civilization on Glorvia IV. Reaching the ruler of said civilization, a creature that resembled a sad compromise between a frog and drafting table, he confirmed that the deal to sign over ninety percent of the treasury in exchange for planetary salvation was still in effect. The king assured him that Glorvia was more than willing to accept miserable poverty rather than suffer the even more miserable humiliation of having the planet eaten by a bunny. Vossoff hesitated, thanks to the familiar chill he always experienced whenever he seemed about to attain everything he ever wanted — a sensation that came from being brutally screwed out of it so many times. He repeated: "Ninety percent. Plus expenses."

"Yes, yes! Only hurry, before my subjects lose all hope! They're already lighting the sacred incense of mass defenestration!"

"Done," said Vossoff. He activated the program.

This was a remarkable moment, unprecedented in the history of the Vossoff/Nimmitz partnership — the first time either one of them had actually succeeded at anything. Because Vossoff and Nimmitz happened by, the giant bunny did change course, the Glorvian civilization was saved, and the Glorvian people did survive to eventually achieve greatness as the exporters of the galaxy's single most malodorous brand of cheese.

Alas, the moment after that was far more typical, as Vossoff waltzed away from the Databank only to be immediately pounced on and eaten.

He didn't realize he'd been pounced on and eaten — the process being so instantaneous that he perceived it as a sudden undignified plunge into a bowl filled with marbles. He said the only thing he could say in such circumstances, which was "Mmmrph!"

Nimmitz cried out to him from the darkness. "Ernst!"

Vossoff managed to fight his way to the surface of the marble sea. "Karl?"

"Ernst!"

"Karl! Where the hell are we?"

"Inside the round thing!" shouted Nimmitz.

"You mean the spherical device with the long protruding rod?"

Somewhere inside the chamber, a tidal wave of marbles shifted position noisily. "Yes! That!"

"And what, may I ask, are we doing inside the spherical device with the long protruding rod?"

"I don't know!" cried Nimmitz. (Marbles jangled together again). "As soon as I got close enough, it rocketed across the deck, opened up, and scooped me in! Then it started driving around looking for you! I've been keeping my head above aggies ever since!"

Vossoff's brain churned furiously. "It must be some kind of maintenance device, designed to pick up after the kid."

"I don't care about that!" hollered Nimmitz. "It's dark in here!"

"Calm down. This is a minor complication at best. We have plenty of time to figure out an escape route so we can return to our ship and collect our obscenely lucrative reward. I promise you, Karl — this time tomorrow, we'll still be wealthy men."

The marbles shifted. "You really think so?"

"Yes, I really think so."

"You sure?"

Vossoff sank a little deeper into the marbles himself. "Frankly, no . . ."

It was sometime later.

The fuzzy pink bunny had left the Glorvian system and was now headed out into interstellar space. Even with state-of-the-art warp capability, it would not arrive anywhere equally interesting for at least one Terran month; its screens would be blank, its ability to entertain its pilot temporarily nil.

As was only fair and reasonable, the autopilot engaged, instantly disconnecting the giant tyke from all command functions, and granting him a break from his reign of destruction.

As was also only fair and reasonable, the pilot blinked, made a noise very much like "goo," and surveyed the command center for something capable of occupying his time until the next planet needed eating.

Very quickly, he spotted something.

He picked up his rattle — a sphere, attached to a protruding rod-shaped handle, which doubled as a maintenance drone whenever not in use — and began to shake it vigorously.

It made most unusual noises. Some of which resembled the gravelly shifting of marbles, some of which an adult of its species might have recognized as yells and grunts and pleas to be let out.

Interlude One

"I am beginning to sense a pattern here," said the spitcurled alien.

The beautiful woman nodded, a simple act that caused sentients of twelve separate species to melt sighing into the suspicious stains on the tablecloths before them. "Yes," she said. "It was a pattern they followed for a long long time, that in fact pre-dated the earliest incident I know about. Ernst led them into a dangerous situation, Ernst painted a huge pattern on concentric circles on the surrounding landscape, Ernst and Karl stood staring up at the sky as a little black mote high above them increased in apparent size and diameter as it plummeting headlong toward their unsuspecting heads. Karl at least still had some sense of self-preservation, in those early days — you'll note that he was always the one who had the bad feeling — but then he also had some brain cells, too, and most of those didn't survive the incident with the bunny."

The pirate alien was off in the corner beating the hapless jukebox with a neutron sledgehammer; though every fifth blow got a protesting, "Ow," he was not willing to stop until he upped that average. "Arrrr. And just when did you come into it?"

"I came into it," the beautiful woman said, "next."

Just a Couple of Pastrami Sandwiches in a Living Room the Size of Infinity

Of the many billions of habitable planets in the galaxy, only five are classified as Perfect: so verdant with life and sunshine and the potential for pure happiness that any sentients who attempt to land on them spontaneously combust with joy just from trying to get too close. Several hundred others are classed Damn Near Perfect: which is to say, they have all the requisite magnificent scenic vistas, and gorgeous climates, and gullibly servile natives, that can make any planet seem like paradise until you discover the one overwhelming flaw that your travel agent inevitably forgot to tell you about — like mosquitoes that drink spinal fluid, or mountain ranges that hop.

Take the privately owned world, Gingrich VII.

From orbit, it doesn't seem like such a horrible place; it has snowcapped mountains and babbling brooks and plentiful resources and the usual assortment of adorably photogenic animal life so accommodating they don't even resent being shot at. But it also has a gravitational anomaly in its core, one that makes it almost impossible to step out onto the surface without immediately becoming re-acquainted with breakfast and lunch. To wit: the gravity fluctuates between 7 and 15 percent every five seconds, precisely duplicating the sensation of riding a boat in choppy water. As a result, sentients who land there spend their entire visits being violently and uncontrollably seasick. They aren't able to eat or sleep or even walk straight; their only desire is a good sturdy railing to be sick over. The local fauna isn't immune, which is one persuasive reason they don't mind being shot at. It is, after all, preferable to living there.

The entire off-worlder population consists of a reclusive but beautiful Terran named Dejah Shapiro, who happens to be one of the wealthiest beings in the known cosmos. She could live anywhere she wanted, but she visited Gingrich VII ten standard years ago and decided she liked the environment just fine.

The newspads attributed this to her iron constitution and unwavering strength of will. The gossip columnists called her just another standard-issue wealthy eccentric. The scientific community theorized about a genetic mutation which rendered her immune to the whoopsies. Her friends understood that, after co-habitation with her ex-husband, life on the Upchuck Planet was a substantial improvement.

At least, until that aforementioned ex-husband, the notorious galactic criminal Ernst Vossoff, showed up at the front door of her sumptuously appointed mansion, with a bouquet of fresh roses in hand and his pale, reeling partner Karl Nimmitz in tow.

It was a close call as to which of the three was most nauseated.

To give Vossoff all due credit, he tried to be suave and debonair even as the disorienting effect of Gingrich VII turned his skin a shade of purple-gray. (In this, he was miles ahead of his partner Nimmitz, who'd quickly crawled into the greenhouse to shiver in misery behind the ferns.) He was gallant, poetic, and contrite; he wore a rented holosuit programmed with the image of the same old-fashioned shiny black tuxedo he'd worn at their wedding; he even turned down the volume on the suit whenever the tuxedo program was interrupted by the usual ten minutes of commercials. But any chances of Dejah actually being taken in were ruined by the obviousness of his desperation, since both he and his partner had the look of men who'd been pounded into a semiliquid mash, baked into a paste, and used for couch stuffing.

She spoke firmly. "Go away, Ernst."

His Stalinesque eyes went all moist and waifish. "How can you be so cold? We were married fifteen years!"

"You only wanted access to my vast interstellar fortune."

"How can you even think that!? I stayed with you long after I checked your bank account and discovered you'd changed the codes!"

"You were married to 15,000 other women at the time."

"And you know very well that that's a misleading figure! They were all members of a Bulgasi Group-Mind Entity, and only shared one consciousness, and therefore can only be counted as one bigamous marriage. Besides, you were my one true love. I only married the 15,000 other women to get the Bulgasi citizenship I needed for my smuggling permit."

"Yes, I was once stupid enough to buy that explanation. But I've since found out that you even cheated on them . . . with the 15,000 members of yet another totally unrelated Bulgasi Group-Mind Entity."

"Those floozies? They came on to me in a bar."

"All 15,000 of them?"

"*You* try saying no when you're so outnumbered!"

Dejah was suddenly afflicted by a highly familiar sensation — that of a foreign object roughly the size and shape of a pineapple springing into existence between her eyes. She hadn't felt anything like it since the last time she'd tried to have a reasonable conversation with Ernst Vossoff. She seized him by his holographic lapels, making the projection flicker in the middle of some alien caterer's commercial for humans on a stick. "Ernst. It's been twenty years. Why . . . are . . . you . . . here?"

He saw the look in her eyes and acquiesced. "I need capital."

"What?"

"For my latest and most brilliant business plan. One that would make Vossoff-Nimmitz Enterprises the kind of fortunes capable of dwarfing even yours. . . . were you not the silent partner raking in half the profits."

"You must think me hydrocephalic. When was the last time you ever had an idea that worked?"

"Never," he said, seriously. "Indeed, my last brilliant scheme ended with poor Nimmitz and I breaking every bone in our bodies and enduring two weeks in an escape-proof spherical chamber where our shattered forms were repeatedly pelted by thousands of ball bearings. And yes, we'd be there still if we hadn't been rescued by the Space Patrol, patched together, put on trial for outstanding warrants, Executed, Revived, Executed Again, Revived Again, and then served six months hard labor in a prison so rough that the rocks regenerated between blows. And indeed, that ordeal, undignified as it was, was not half as bad as what befell us upon the failure of the scheme before that.

But don't you see? That's the whole point. Since, whatever else you might think of me, you are well aware of my superior intelligence, you must also recognize that all of these failures were due to factors well beyond my control. Bad luck, in other words. And that, my dear, means The Law of Averages is ticking."

Dejah was appalled to realize that it made sense. She owed most of her own far-flung fortune to her keen understanding of the laws of Probability and Chance . . . and much as she hated to admit it, nobody could lose as frequently and as spectacularly as Ernst Vossoff without threatening the very structure of the universe; The Law of Averages owed him a Holy Grail, a Ring of Power, a Magic Carpet, a Genie in a Lamp, a Winning Lottery Ticket, a four-leaf clover, a Pristine Mint Copy of the incredibly rare and spectacularly valuable *Anvil-Man Comics #1*, a Lucky Star, a tax exemption, a Pot of Gold at the End of the Rainbow, and a Home Run With Two Men Out and Three Men On. Wealthy as she was, she couldn't afford to *not* listen to his idea . . .

Too, there was the ungodly plaintive wailing of Karl Nimmitz, who was still in the greenhouse, futilely begging the entire planet to stop playing games with his gag reflex. It really was the most pathetic sound Dejah Shapiro had ever heard. Well, maybe not the absolute *most* pitiful sound; Ernst had, after all, insisted on singing at their wedding. But it definitely belonged in the top five. And — now that she listened more closely — its lost, helpless quality moved a part of her that she'd thought forever buried.

Was it greed, or something else, that motivated her decision? "All right. The Guest Parlor's equipped with Quantum Dampeners, so my infrequent guests can discuss business without crippling gastrointestinal distress. Help me bring your friend in there, before he makes a mess, and

I'll consider anything you have to say."

"Who knows?" cried Vossoff. "This might even be the first step toward a reconciliation —"

She tittered delicately, placed a soft, elegantly manicured hand on his trembling shoulder, and kneed him in the groin. "Correction. Almost anything."

Dejah Shapiro's Guest Parlor was the single gaudiest living room in the entire history of the universe. She'd accomplished this by installing trans-dimensional receders in the infrastructure, warping all the rules of geometry and tasteful decorating to render the room literally infinite in its dimensions. The fastest starship ever constructed could be launched off the ottoman and require millions of years to reach the fireplace. Fortunately for the sanity of everybody who ever visited her, all the usable furniture occupied a scenic mountaintop only a few kilometers from the entranceway, so party guests didn't have to exceed the speed of light every time they wanted to refresh the ice in their drinks.

Dejah was petty enough to leave Vossoff at the vestibule with a map and a good pair of hiking shoes, while she chauffeured the still recovering Nimmitz to the living room set in a land speeder kept there for that very purpose. Almost as soon as they peeled out, Nimmitz stuck his head out the window to catch the wind on his face, his big floppy tongue lolling.

Dejah pressed her the tip of her forefinger to the dimple in her chin. "That's interesting. I've seen Golden Retrievers and Stygian Blood-Slugs do that, but never a grown man."

Nimmitz's tongue lashed him in the face. "Mmmmrrrppph."

"How incredibly cosmopolitan. Do you behave this

way often?"

He pulled himself back in through the window. "Well, not out in interplanetary space, ma'am. I'd get sucked out by the vacuum."

"Yes, I suppose you would. But aside from that, Karl — it is Karl, right? — whenever you're on a planetary surface, being chauffeured to an important business meeting by a wealthy and glamorous potential investor, then you act like Fido? Am I correct in that assumption?"

"Uh huh." And his head went out the window again, forcing Dejah to swerve hard to the left just to avoid painting a nearby rock outcropping with his face.

"Ah well. I was wondering what kind of man would willingly enter a business partnership with Ernst Vossoff, and now I guess I know. — How did you two hook up, anyway?"

"We were chained together in a mining prison," he said. "On Bungertuis III. He was serving an eternal life sentence for selling an entire sentient race into slavery —"

Dejah's long, graceful fingers tightened on the wheel. "Oh, no! I didn't know about that one! Please tell me that even Ernst Vossoff, the fiend who used to shear off and sell my hair for mattress stuffing as I slept, wouldn't sink that low!"

"Well, he didn't mean to, ma'am. But he didn't know they were sentient; they were in the dormant stage of their life cycle and they weren't moving around. All he knew is that they were small and hairy and lying around by the millions, waiting to be picked up. And they were just the right size and color to be shipped off to the Shatnerians as custom toupees —"

"Aaaarrrggghhhh. Say no more. And you, Karl? What were you in for?"

"Breaking into a gumball machine."

"No! Really?"

"I wanted a red," explained Nimmitz.

"And for that, they chain you to a notorious con-man and galactic slaver?"

"I guess so. The Bungertians take their chewing gum seriously. They consider it a symbol of everything that's good and decent."

"And what did Ernst, who takes such pride in being such an alleged criminal genius, have to say about being chained to a petty thief whose biggest accomplishment to date had been robbing a gumball machine?"

"He said it was a splendid opportunity," Nimmitz replied. "He said that if I escaped with him and became his sniveling lackey, the worthless uncomprehending toad who sat still for all his abuse and exposition, he would teach me how to become a brilliantly cunning master criminal like him."

Dejah gazed upon the hairless, slow-talking man in the passenger seat, her expression profoundly troubled for the first time. "And has it worked out that way, Karl?"

"Well, not really," Nimmitz admitted. "It's been twenty years, and I'm still a sniveling lackey. In fact, he hasn't even told me what he's planning now. But don't forget, we spent ten of those years rooted to a wall on New Pylthothi after being transformed to a previously extinct form of smelly alien moss."

That did it. Dejah tore off a hunk of steering wheel and popped it, sans condiments, into her mouth. Beside her, Nimmitz hollered; she didn't bother explaining to him that she'd had the entire vehicle constructed of a light sedative, which could be swallowed one piece at a time to alleviate driving stress.

She was suddenly certain that she'd be needing the entire dashboard, to deal with whatever Vossoff had to propose . . .

...between the stripping of the pleasantly narcotic land speeder, and the multiple cocktails they also downed while waiting, Dejah and Nimmitz were totally looped by the time Vossoff reached them. They'd been watching his slow and laborious approach for quite some time, and were by that point relaxed enough to place friendly wagers on the number of welts he'd get from the swarm of stinger-bugs he accidentally disturbed halfway up the mountain. (Nimmitz actually made more money on this bet than he had since escaping from the chain gang with Vossoff; but then Dejah, who was secretly controlling the bugs with a remote secreted in her palm, deliberately let him. She was really getting to like Nimmitz.)

Upon reaching the summit, Vossoff gave them the kind of glare that's been declared illegal on a hundred different planets. "Very funny, Dejah. I mean, I'm just laughing out loud here. Do you want to hear my proposal or don't you?"

Dejah batted her eyes. "I'm sorry, Ernst. You're right, of course. Speak your piece."

"All right," said Vossoff. He sat on the edge of the recliner, plucked a cluster of stinger-bug quills from the tip of his tongue, and began: "Imagine the most valuable substance in the universe. Something that fills the thoughts and dreams of countless souls all across the galaxy. Something so important that billions think of nothing else, so valuable that billions expend fortunes to make themselves its master, so dangerous that billions have died from being unable to conquer it, and yet so common that we cannot step into a corner deli without unintentionally acquiring a generous supply. Yes, my dear esteemed colleagues, I am describing —"

An invisible light bulb went off over Nimmitz's head. "Pastrami!"

Dejah suppressed a giggle.

Vossoff's dark brown eyes radiated hate in his partner's direction. "No, my friend, I am not discussing Pastrami, though in your usual idiotic manner you have come tantalizingly close —"

"Corned Beef!" Nimmitz shouted.

Dejah didn't suppress the next giggle at all. It just poured out of her, loud enough to fill a thousand living rooms the size of the cosmos. . . . and it felt so good she wondered why she didn't do it more often. Probably because she'd never had anybody like Nimmitz around before. "No, Karl. I think he's describing Fat."

"Exactly!" Vossoff shouted maniacally, literally jumping up and down with glee at the novelty of once again encountering somebody smart enough to know what he was talking about. "You do understand! It's everywhere! Every intelligent vertebrate is prone to it, every sentient race suffers from it! Every planet that's achieved a comfortable level of civilization also sports an excess of weighty avoirdupois! Indeed, if you look through a galactic almanac sometime, you'll probably discover that there are more pot-bellies in the universe than there are heads!" He addressed Nimmitz. "Don't you see what I'm saying, Karl? Don't you?"

On the spot, Nimmitz did the best he could. "Maybe — the people with the big pot bellies are eating the people with the heads."

"No, I'm not saying that, you bubble-brained buffoon. I'm saying it's a universal constant, like entropy or gravity or your own inability to substantially warm the inside of your skull with your brain. I'm saying that it exists all over the known galaxy. And while most sentients are so anxious to get rid of it that they subject themselves to indignities like diets and mind control and face-projection implants and positronic governors, a substantial number of other sentients actually prize it as a badge of status and prosperity, and gorge themselves with unlimited quantities of high-calorie food in a vain attempt to accrue the mass that their high metabolisms won't let them gain. In short, you little cranial turnip, I'm saying it's just a simple matter of Supply and Demand — the essential basis of capitalism all over the cosmos!"

The dense incomprehension Nimmitz radiated in all directions made Dejah's little pocket universe flicker at the edges. At length — which is to say, sometime before the stars above went cold — his eyes widened with sudden understanding. "You want to open a drive-through Fat place!"

"That would be redundant, dear," said Dejah, gently patting him on the wrist for at least making the attempt. She turned back to Vossoff. "Continue."

"What I suggest," Vossoff continued, in the manner of a man reciting a long-rehearsed speech, "is nothing less than the combined application of two separate highly advanced technologies — nanotech and instantaneous matter transmission — in a manner so revolutionary that the galactic stock market might as well just up shop and hand us the keys, so we can claim all the spare change. Because, while the means exist, nobody's ever built a microscopic matter transmission system before. Nobody's ever seen the point. Up until now, matter transmission's only been good for getting on and off starships so poorly designed they have no way to land. But," and here he stabbed a finger in the air, as if attempting to assassinate the stars, "if we construct nanobots capable of entering one organism and genetically reconfiguring unwanted fat cells for instantaneous transmission into another organism that has use for them —"

Dejah got it. "Oh . . . my . . . God. We'd be able to charge for weight loss and weight gain at the same time."

Nimmitz said, "Can we have some Pastrami later?"

Vossoff dismissed him and addressed all his attention to Dejah. "Now, if you will, calculate a reasonable surcharge for each individual kilo of mass we transmit across the cosmos. Multiply that by ten billion inhabited planets, each possessing an average of one billion intelligent sentients uncomfortable with their own body weight, and assume, just for the sake of argument, that only one world in ten thousand agrees to avail itself of our unique services. How rich would we be, dearest?"

"I haven't had pastrami in years," Nimmitz suddenly realized.

Dejah opened her mouth, certain that she was about to come up with the objection that would prove Vossoff's plan the evil, self-destructive nonsense that his plans had always been before. But she couldn't speak. Vossoff's idea was not only audacious, brilliant, and so simple that her pet engineers could slap together the necessary technology in a matter of hours — it was also the kind of once-in-a-millennium advance in the field of medicine that would leave her, Vossoff and Nimmitz revered figures for all time.

What's more, it didn't screw anybody. The thin people got to be as fat as they wanted and the fat people got to be as thin as they wanted. Nobody got taken, nobody got victimized, nobody was left shaking his fist at a receding space-skimmer as Ernst Vossoff escaped with his ill-gotten loot.

Something was wrong.

Or, as the great Terran law-enforcement official, Elliot Ness, once said to his most famous quarry, the gangster Al Capone: "Al, if it weren't a crime, you wouldn't be interested."

Disturbed, she said, "Go on."

Vossoff twirled the tip of his walrus moustache. "Right now, there are thousands of entire sentient species on the dole because they don't have the resources or the know-man who calls himself a Junior Space Ranger, but is widely rumored to be royalty in exile. She flies a air-skimmer over the soft, fleshy, jiggling, terrain, more like skin than planetary geology, and cheerfully points out the odd acoustical anomaly which has rendered the mountain the number-one tourist attraction for visitors to this quadrant: namely, the way the prevailing winds insist on sounding exactly like an enraged man shrieking incessant curses in Slavic. Her husband always scratches his head and furrows his brow, distantly aware that he's heard the sound somewhere else, but unable to recall exactly when. She always kisses him and says, that's all right, my sweet, it really doesn't matter.

Of course, she never shows him the eastern side of the mountain, where the critical clue sits between two balloon-cheeks the size of houses.

Namely: a wide-open shouting mouth.

And the shaggy, unkempt remains of a walrus moustache.

Interlude Two

The spitcurled alien, who had turned suddenly green, gagged, moved went over to the jukebox and baptized it with a multicolored march down the digestive memory lane. It wasn't the first time it had been decorated in this manner by Ralphs patrons who had had too much to imbibe; that had been happening every five minutes for years. It was, however, the first time the alien in question was a creature with an internal temperature above the melting point of lead. The jukebox glowed white-hot in protest, playing a Lief Garrett just to show it couldn't be pushed around.

Then somebody hit it with a chair until it said, "Ow."

The spitcurled alien then returned to his previous seat and said, "Eccch."

"That's all right," Dejah said. "It happens to everybody. You just have to learn to hold your liquor, that's all."

The spitcurled alien glared. "It has nothing to do with liquor."

"Oh."

"It's just revulsion."

"Oh? You think I treated him poorly?"

"No. I think you did the right thing. That's not the problem."

"What's the problem?"

"The problem," the spitcurled alien said, "is that I spent one entire vacation climbing that mountain."

"Oh, dear."

"Barehanded."

"You poor thing."

"Making my approach," the spitcurled alien cried, a vein in his temple throbbing, "up a narrow fissure that I mistakenly believed to be a fjord!"

The line that formed to abuse the jukebox, upon this announcement, stretched out the door and into the swamp, where several unwary patrons were eaten by gators.

Just a Couple of Highly Experimental Weapons Tucked Away Behind the Toilet Paper

Recovering from severe mental trauma in an advanced interstellar civilization can be more difficult than it sounds... especially when the other patients on your ward include carnivorous lizard-things with transparent skulls, shuffling blobs of semi-liquid goo who shoot acid at three-second intervals, and soulful-eyed marsupians who carry their own digestive organs around with them in buckets.

The problem is not simply that some of these creatures are alien enough to shatter your already delicate psyche, it's that you cannot regain your grip on reality at all without first figuring out which of them are really there and which are just your playful subconscious having fun with you. You can waste years in such an institution, gradually learning to accept that the giant slug which keeps trying to eat you during group therapy is just a delusional manifestation of your deep-rooted childhood resentment toward your sweet little silver-haired mother, only to find out after multiple shock treatments that you are in fact a giant slug yourself, and that you never had a sweet little silver-haired mother except as an appetizer.

Under the circumstances, it's easy to see why folks who go insane in advanced interstellar civilizations usually remain that way.

In the case of that notorious interstellar criminal Ernst Vossoff, who had spent the better part of the past three years in the incurable ward obsessively cutting out paper dolls, giving them names, and using them to reenact the Napoleonic Wars in brutally realistic campaigns that left the floor of his padded cell ankle-deep in confetti, he remained a conscientious objector to reality until the day his principal therapist oozed in through the heating vent and spoke kindly supportive words through the prosthetic Sigmund Freud head it held between its multiple rows of razor-sharp teeth. "Ernst, my boy! How are we doing today?"

"Am I Abraham Lincoln?" drooled Vossoff. "I think I'm Abraham Lincoln. I used to be Genghis Khan, but then John Wayne got the part. Why can't gravity be less of a law and more of a gentle suggestion? Kenneth, what is the frequency? Goo goo ga joob."

"Excellent," said the therapist, who naturally came from an alien culture where pointless non-sequiturs were considered the soul of wit; he'd spent years training Vossoff to make absolutely no sense whatsoever, and he personally thought that the Earthman had made almost enough progress to be released into the community. "I've been directed to tell you that you have a visitor."

"Salvador Dali once dated a moon goddess. There are fourteen l's in the word kangaroo. Why isn't republicanism an adverb? Blonctspotch McGillicuddy, I've got a bunion."

The therapist beamed (literally, since his race emitted laser fire when happy). "Absolutely. I'll let him in."

And so he oozed out of the way as the door irised open to admit a singularly unusual specimen of terrain-strain humanity. Aforementioned specimen being a burly, hairless, moist-eyed thug whose expression was not incredibly far from the perpetual incomprehension native to the faces of toy poodles.

All of Vossoff's painstakingly installed nonsense conditioning melted away in a single instant. He shrieked, *"You!!!!,"* burst his strait-jacket, and leaped across the cell, his hands already spasmodically twitching in anticipation of their fatal grip on the neck of his traitorous ex-partner Karl Nimmitz. But even as the murderous Slav made contact, Nimmitz pressed the larger of two buttons on a small device in his right hand, and both men vanished . . . perplexing the squidlike therapist that he actually swallowed his prosthetic Sigmund Freud head in a single gulp.

The therapist was, by the way, later proven to be one of Vossoff's delusions. But that was okay. His success rate with the other patients was so high that he was still permitted to practice medicine.

A s for Vossoff, he was not quite in the mood to interpret this as a rescue. He stood on the gleaming control decks of Nimmitz's brand-new top of the line space cruiser, immobilized by an automatic ship's security stasis field, threatening bloody revenge at the imbecilic ex-partner smiling at him from the opposite side of the control room.

"I will murder you," Vossoff ranted. "I will expunge you from existence. I will render this universe a place where you never lived. I will travel back in time and unplug the refrigeration unit on the fetus vending machine that spawned you. I will travel back still further, seek out the mother of the demented genius who invented the technology, and persuade her to forego parenting in favor of a career dancing in alien ballets. I will travel back still further than that, and force-feed her great-great-grandparents mind-altering drugs so they think they're different species and thus never fall in love or mate; and from there I will travel to the very earliest beginnings of evolution on your wretched homeworld, and stomp down hard on the first trilobite I see crawling from the primordial muck!"

"Gee," Nimmitz said, with his characteristic lack of irony. "I thought you'd be happier to see me."

"You Paleolithic putz! You married my hated ex-wife, let her steal the fruits of my genius, and raised not one peep of objection as she transformed me into a mound of fat the size of a mountain range!"

Nimmitz blinked so many times in the next second that his eyelids almost opened a gateway to another space-time continuum. "Gosh. I guess I do owe you an apology for that one. I mean, I did marry Dejah, and we're very happy together, but I honestly didn't know about that mound of fat part. Although, come to think of it, it does sound like the kind of thing she would do. How on Vlhan did you get changed back to normal?"

"It didn't happen on Vlhan, you backstabbing baboon! And never mind how I managed it! It's enough that I spent the last three years recovering from the psychic trauma! And when I get my hands on you and that traitorous little trollop, I'll —"

A multitude of voices behind Vossoff interjected in unison. "... be rich beyond your wildest dreams of avarice."

Vossoff whirled, expecting a mob, finding instead a single alien creature of a species he had never personally encountered before: one that could have been described as an old-fashioned coffee table bearing dozens of tiny, grinning, multi-fanged fish heads in upside-down bell jars. It took him a second to see that the table was in fact wholly organic, that the heads were all attached to it, and that the legs were sinuous prehensile tails lined with moist wriggling cilia. The upside-down bell jars were evidently some sort of breathing mechanism, providing the beast with its version of a planetary atmosphere, which suited Vossoff just fine, as he was instantly grateful to not be sharing his own precious oxygen with such a thing.

Still, Ernst Vossoff being who and what he was, it took him only half a heartbeat to cut past the strangeness of the alien's appearance, to the heart and soul of what it had said. And then he grinned, and twirled the tips of his walrus moustache, and spoke with sudden deceptive calm. "Ohhhh, I wouldn't know about that. My wildest dreams of avarice are rather unrealistically grandiose."

"So we've been told," said the collection of heads. "Indeed, all of our exhaustive research into your background confirms you to be an appallingly single-minded specimen of the peculiar human subgroup known as 'greedy bastards'. Nevertheless, we feel perfectly justified in asserting that even you cannot possibly underestimate the extent of the riches we offer you."

"Really? Not even if I want, say," Vossoff made a big show of trying to come up with just one random idea off the top of his head, "a mercenary army powerful enough to crush all opposition, raze everything in its path, conquer the galaxy and install me as official emperor and god?"

The collection of heads waggled its cilia disparagingly. "Pfah! Pocket change! We thought you had more ambition than that!"

Vossoff tapped his lips with the tip of his index finger. "Interesting," he said finally, in the kind of disparaging tone designed to show how little he meant it. "And would I have to share these ill-gotten gains with my mindless oaf of an ex-partner, who so ungratefully left me suffocating beneath billions of tons of quivering cellulite?"

Nimmitz cried out: *"Hey!"*

"The answer to your question," said the collection of heads, "is no. The wealth and power would all be yours. All Mr. Nimmitz wants out of this deal is to get his beloved wife back. In short, Dejah Shapiro is missing, and we feel that you are the only man in her life even remotely sentient enough to find her."

Once again, Nimmitz cried: *"Hey!"*

Vossoff grinned. "So. Let me see if I have this straight. If I agree, I get to rule the galaxy like a God. If I refuse, my ex-wife remains missing and is never heard from again. Is that, minor explanatory details notwithstanding, essentially the difficult choice you are offering me?"

"Essentially," said the collection of heads, "yes. Except that it wouldn't be this galaxy, but another one identical to it in every way."

Vossoff chewed on that. Chewed on it some more. Tapped his foot while continuing to think about it further. Almost opened his mouth to speak, then stopped and simply paced back and forth. He was imitating a set of scales with his outstretched palms, raising first one, then the other, but seemingly either unwilling or unable to make them balance out to anything other than perfect equilibrium, when an anguished Nimmitz cried out: "Oh, come *on*, Ernst! That isn't fair!"

It was twenty minutes later. Vossoff had washed up, shaved, and dressed in a fresh jumpsuit befitting the criminal mastermind that he was. He and Nimmitz now sat side-by-side in the control room, listening to the alien's spiel.

The collection of heads turned out to be a renowned physicist from a major university on a planet that translated as {the sound of water being absorbed by desert sand}. His own name translated as {the sound of water being violently expelled by desert sand, which on its planet is a silicon-based intelligence that cannot abide the taste}. Inevitably, he used to be teased about the name as a crècheling, was inevitably saddled with the insulting nickname {Mudsplat}, and had to suffer through such traumas as the time in the neighborhood vomitorium when —

"Get on with it," growled Vossoff.

{Mud}'s cilia trembled in broken-hearted annoyance. "I am beginning to realize why so many of your people consider you a real jerk, but very well. — We (that is to say, not just the group-entity standing before you, but an assortment of other qualified group-entities much like us who functioned as our peers in this project), have recently invented a cure for unhappiness."

Vossoff leaned back in his chair and rested his chin on his own interlocked fingers. "So have I. It's called obscenely vast quantities of wealth and power."

"Frankly, we believe so, too, but merely recognizing that won't persuade other sentients to freely provide us with either. Therefore, we have designed an entirely new technology which we believe will swell our coffers considerably. It's called the Alternatrix, and it's essentially a doorway into alternate universes . . ."

"Oh, puh-lease!" Vossoff derided, with a dismissive wave of his hand. "Don't tell me that's your big mysterious scheme! Interdimensional travel has been old hat for years!"

"We are aware of that, Mr. Vossoff, just as we are aware that it's never been rendered practical. The time and energy involved in sifting through the literally infinite number of alternate universes has long been the major stumbling block preventing anybody from finding those that substantially improve on this one. After all, alternate universes are not labeled, or for that matter, arranged in any coherent order — one can waste entire eons struggling to identify the unique quality of a universe that differs from ours only in the precise position of an individual thumbtack on a departmental bulletin board in the regional tax offices of an obscure planet otherwise known only for the rubbery taste of its pasta. And indeed, I did not come up with that particular example just out of thin air, since before we came up with our breakthrough, our project founder, the venerable Professor {sound of granite hillside eroding into shape of terrestrial carrot}, did drop dead of shock when, after cataloguing over 200,000 separate universes where the thumbtacks on said bulletin board varied no more than a couple of centimeters in one direction or another, he finally located a plane where the office staff had used staples instead."

"Staples?" cried Nimmitz. "The fiends!"

{Mud} froze in mid-expression, staring at the horrified Nimmitz, unable to parse the precise relevance of his interruption. After a moment, he shuddered with several dozen heads at once, and continued: "It's clear that most alternate universes are not even worth the time and effort of exploration; they're like theme parks to irrelevant diversity. The problem has long been the difficulty in developing an intelligent filtering mechanism, capable of taking your specifications for the precise kind of alternate universe you wish to find, and then instantaneously scanning the myriad dimensions for the one that fits your description. This, sir, is our Alternatrix."

Vossoff brushed his moustache. "So, if I asked you — purely as an illustration, mind you — to find me a universe where science fiction editors mate with vending machines, dentists are required by law to daily beat their thumbs with hammers, and a secret conspiracy of professional wrestlers was responsible for the assassination of the twentieth-century American president John F. Kennedy . . ."

"I would ask you whether you meant masked or unmasked wrestlers."

"And if I replied, 'masked'?"

"I would ask Olympic, Mexican, or World Federation. Trust me, sir . . . you cannot name an alternate universe so ridiculous that our Alternatrix is not capable of finding it. Which is how we can promise you a galactic empire: we know we can find a universe willing to accept you as ruler."

Vossoff thought about that, smiled, and cracked his knuckles. "And just how did you intend to use this as a cure for unhappiness?"

"The Alternatrix reads its subject's brain-waves and automatically opens a portal to the parallel universe most likely to strike any individual as paradise."

"And I suppose you will require people to sign over all their money and property before taking this one-way trip?"

{Mud} snorted. "Of course. We're not doing this because we're fuzzyheaded liberals. We have a profit motive here."

"And how can they know you're not simply transporting them into the center of a sun and pocketing the money? It's what I would do."

"Because we won't make them sign the papers until they've returned from a one-month free trip to see whether it's really what they want. By then, they're desperate to sign. It's all very above-board, really. And a sure-fire moneymaker, since nobody's ever really been satisfied with the universe they were born in. We foresee a 50,000 percent profit within the first standard year of operation, but we don't actually have the funds to launch this exciting new enterprise on the interstellar scale it requires. Which is frankly why we met with your ex-wife. who as you know, happens to be one of the three wealthiest individual sentients in the known universe . . ."

". . . and who is now missing," Vossoff concluded.

"Correct."

Vossoff tapped his chin thoughtfully. "You need not continue. You have already given me enough information to reconstruct the events that led to the dear woman going AWOL. You offered her a taste of her ideal universe as a demonstration prior to investment."

"Correct."

"Nimmitz, here, interrupted just long enough to make an irrelevant, and no doubt mind-bogglingly stupid remark."

Nimmitz stirred. "Hey."

{Mud}'s collected heads shuddered at the memory. "Indeed, the inane contents of his contribution still send shock waves reverberating throughout our culture. We are hoping to spend much of our first year's profits on genomat treatments so we can evolve hands and slap our collective foreheads in astonishment."

Nimmitz said, "Hey."

"No doubt," Vossoff persisted, "whatever he said had something to do with pastrami."

"Please. Don't reconstruct it. It's already driven my podmates and egglings to mutual defenestration."

Vossoff nodded sympathetically. "And you don't know how many years I actually *lived* with that. — Dejah used some pretext to trick you into leaving the room, quickly reprogrammed the Alternatrix, and immediately sent herself to some unknown alternate universe of her own choosing, scrambling the database so she could hide on that plane indefinitely without you or your people ever being able to find her, retrieve her, and finalize the agreement that would make the transfer of all her collected wealth legal and binding."

"All correct."

"You need me, as the only sentient man in her life . . ."

Nimmitz rose up out of his chair. *"Hey! Hey hey hey*

hey!"

"... to figure out which, out of the literally infinite number of alternate universes she might have chosen for herself, is the one where she's hiding, so you can yank her out of there, threaten to bar her from that particular paradise should she not choose to ante up, get her signatures on your contracts, claim her entire fortune, and commence building your business empire."

Two dozen fish heads nodded vigorously enough to set their little bell jars chiming at high pitch. "An astounding set of deductions, sir."

"As a certain famous ancestor of mine once said," Vossoff replied, twirling his walrus moustache with self-congratulatory aplomb, "Elementary." He bowed. "May I respectfully ask that you permit my ex-partner and I some time alone on this matter? I'm certain that as the two great loves of Dejah's life, we will be able to come up with some helpful epiphanies."

Dozens of alien lizard-heads regarded Nimmitz doubtfully. "Do you truly believe he'll be any help? On our way here, when we were cruising hyperspace at fifteen times the speed of light, he actually tried to step outside with a flashlight to see what would happen when he turned on the beam."

"Interesting. I honestly believed I'd long since talked him out of that experiment. Nevertheless, one of the wealthiest, most desirable, most lusted-after woman in the known universe has inexplicably given him her heart, so there must be a semblance of coherent electrical activity going on in that absurdly-designed head of his. If nothing else, he will be invaluable in helping to isolate the wrong answers."

"Very well," {Mud} said doubtfully, as he scuttled away on his many elegantly varnished legs. Few creatures in the universe, with the possible exception of middle-aged

Terran accountants in horizontally striped bathing suits, would have looked more absurd leaving a room. Vossoff watched him go with his glad-handing smile firmly in place — and a heretofore unseen resolve just beginning to well in his cruel Stalinesque face.

Nimmitz wiped a tear from the corner of his moist puppylike eyes. "Do you really think you can find her, Ernst? I miss her an awful lot."

"I cannot make any promises, you humanoid gerbil. It has, after all, been several decades since she and I were pronounced man and harpy. I never truly understood her even then, and the special laws of thermodynamics that govern shrewish ex-wives provide any number of revolting ways that she might have become even more incomprehensible in the interim. Indeed, she would have had to, to honestly prefer you over me."

Nimmitz said, "She used to laugh in bed about the way you —"

"Yes, yes, yes, I'm certain it was very cute and made me look woefully inadequate. But that is irrelevant now. What is relevant is that I fully understand why the dear woman seized the opportunity to hide. She clearly recognized our foes for what they are: one of the greatest threats ever to face the known universe."

Nimmitz goggled. "Huh?"

Vossoff slapped his forehead. "She must have been happy with you for *some* reason . . . tell me, how frequently do you two make love?"

"Monday through Friday."

"You make love five times a week?"

Nimmitz blinked. "No, just once. Monday through Friday."

Vossoff weighed the image, shuddered meaningfully,

then hurried moved on. "In any event, as I started to say before your personal IQ famine forced that annoying detour, it's perfectly clear to me why Dejah went into hiding. She knew that if she didn't try out the Alternatrix, then {Mud} would find some way to force her, in the hopes that she'd emerge from her personal perfect paradise brainwashed and eager to sign over her entire fortune in exchange for passage back. She knew that her fortune would enable these ambulatory Chippendales to establish their enterprise on a galactic scale, that few sentient creatures would be able to resist the siren call of paradise, and that entire star-spanning empires would happily hand over all their collective wealth just to buy their populations billions of individual one-way tickets to Never-Never Land. The galaxy would be depopulated in a few short years, leaving it by default the sole property of {Mud} and his fellow knick-knack tables."

Nimmitz scratched the top of his preternaturally smooth head. "Would that be a bad thing, though? Everybody would still get to live in paradise."

"A surprisingly good point, coming from a cretin who normally only has points at the top of his head. Were I of a certain philosophical bent, I would respond with a pretentious Shatnerian speech about life not having any meaning without first having to fight and suffer and endure great hardships for every fleeting scrap of happiness, blah blah blah, but frankly, Karl, that philosophy always seemed like a bunch of horseshit to me, as I'd frankly much prefer obscenely vast quantities of wealth and power and happiness all handed to me on a silver platter. No, personally, what keeps me, and I strongly suspect Dejah, from eagerly buying a one-way ticket through their device is the knowledge that the coffee tables haven't preceded us up that particular stairway to heaven."

As usual, Nimmitz was fourteen steps behind him.

"Huh?"

"Think for once! They already have a working prototype; they can simply use it themselves instead of exploiting it commercially. Instead, they're staying right here, on this plane of existence, happily plotting a universal conquest that depends entirely upon the rest of galactic civilization rushing where they themselves refuse to tread. This, my planarian friend, is as conducive to trust as entering an allegedly gourmet restaurant and spotting the chef in the back, furtively scarfing a meal of greasy fast-food from just up the block — i.e., if his own food is as incredibly wonderful as advertised, then why is he clogging his arteries with the ordinary slop the proletariat eats?"

"I know!" Nimmitz shouted, happy to contribute for once. "Because he likes to do the connect-the-dots puzzles on the place mats!"

Vossoff froze in mid-dissertation, as usual thrown off-course by his ex-partner's inimitable manner of cutting to the meat of a problem. He blinked several times in rapid succession, and then for several seconds emitted an excruciating grinding noise that might have been the sound of a recently derailed train of thought being forcibly returned to its previous set of tracks. "I infer from the generally humanoid design of the furnishings that this ship belongs to you?"

"Dejah. Her personal yacht. She doesn't let me drive."

"Smart woman. I also infer that our friend with the unpronounceable name doesn't let you drive either?"

"Oh, sure," said Nimmitz. "He brought along a platoon of heavily-armed commandos from his homeworld, and they've switched all navigation and control functions to a secondary control room behind the Pachinko parlor. They did that just after they won the battle and seized the ship. Did I forget to tell you that?"

"That's all right," Vossoff replied. "I'm sure that I

would have figured out we were prisoners sometime after they resorted to questioning under torture. — Tell me, you monument to the gods of ineptitude, where does Dejah keep her weapons locker? Not, mind you, the big shiny one no doubt marked Weapons Locker that she filled with ominous-looking but nonfunctional phonies that hijackers like our friends the coffee tables are intended to find . . . but the hidden cache of genuine top-of-the-line hardware that are honestly meant to be used?"

"In the bathroom. Behind the toilet paper dispenser. Dejah says she put it there so I'll think twice about leaving the seat up."

Vossoff shook his head, overcome with fond memories of an argument that he and Dejah had once fought over that very controversy. It had raged for most of their honeymoon, and resulted in each of them eventually hiring mercenary soldiers to enforce their own point of view. The open warfare had destroyed ancient civilizations on fifty separate star-systems. He shook his head, to clear away the happy reminiscences, and said: "Come on. We have some coffee tables to polish off."

The first law of internal security on a starship is to have a reasonable sense of proportion vis-à-vis the need for superior firepower. For instance, it does you no absolutely no good to fire an all-powerful Bettelhine Munitions Destructo-Beam through the palpitating hearts of the slavering carnivorous mutant advancing down the corridor toward you, if said Destructo-Beam emerges undiminished from said mutant's back and proceeds to punch a tunnel the size of an orange through all twenty layers of your outer hull. Far from it, for even though you currently exceed the size and shape of an orange, explosive decompression will still succeed in improvising a way to fit you through that hole. No; if you must regularly fight pitched battles in the corridors of your starship, it is best to equip yourself with weaponry that can incapacitate your enemy without making an orange out of you.

With that in mind, Vossoff and Nimmitz armed themselves and began their offensive.

They encountered their first alien coffee table in the corridor immediately outside the main control room. He was a tough customer, something Vossoff recognized because all the heads in the little bell jars had eye patches and dueling scars, and also because all four of the table legs were marked with animated holographic tattoos of alien supermodels doing obscene things to fluffy pink bunnies. When the beast saw Vossoff and Nimmitz he cried out and reached for his blasters. Vossoff deftly fired his Bettelhine Munitions Trivia Gun, which promptly rendered the beast unable to think of anything more pressing than who played the lovable time otter Brooklyn in the 2387 holo-series *Have Black Hole Will Dilate*.

That set the alarm claxons sounding, and in seconds fourteen other alien coffee tables scurried around the corner, their blasters waving. Against them Vossoff used his Bettelhine Munitions Psionic Muzak Bomb, which upon exploding immediately filled the corridor surrounding the aliens with obscenely bastardized versions of their favorite songs. The mob immediately fell to the deck, writhing and moaning in unimaginable aesthetic agony. Vossoff and Nimmitz stepped over the pathetic convulsing forms and moved on.

The third and final obstacle greeted them at the portal to the Pachinko parlor. It was an alien coffee table that oddly enough carried no specialized weaponry at all — instead, it was clad in an all-concealing black slipcover that to Vossoff's expert eyes instantly marked it as its civilization's nearest equivalent to a master ninja. Its war cry resembled the sound a cinderblock makes when thrown from a great height into a porcelain bowl filled with cats. Acting with the speed of thought itself, Vossoff whipped out his Bettelhine Munitions Poor Self-Image Generator, which instantly caused the alien martial artist to slink off into a neutral corner to dwell at great length on the bad impression he always made on people.

"I can't believe this!" Nimmitz gasped excitedly, as he and Vossoff reloaded in a nearby utility niche. "We're actually winning! Since when does that happen?"

"Since I first hooked up with you?" asked Vossoff. "Absolutely never."

"Maybe our luck's changing. You used to say we were straining the law of averages to the breaking point; maybe it's finally kicked in."

"Maybe. And maybe the entire universe will put a paper bag over its head and breathe deeply as a cure for entropy."

Nevertheless, as soon as the last door between the two space rogues and the backup control room irised open, both Vossoff and Nimmitz courageously leaped through, their Bettelhine Munitions You Can't Shoot Me, You've Just Had a Crisis of Conscience generators cocked and ready —

— only to trip a proximity-activated Teleportation Grid that ensnared them the second they passed through the door. A brief moment of blissful nonexistence later, both men found themselves re-integrated inside a pair of humanoid-sized Stasis Fields that imprisoned them beside a huge pulsating archway labeled ALTERNATRIX in neon Dom Casual. {Mud} capered at the far end of the chamber, tinkering with the controls; he did not bother to turn around, but he did chuckle evilly, in a particularly snotty way that strongly reminded Vossoff of himself. "You know," he remarked, conversationally, "it's funny. There are any number of embarrassing things that can befall an unlucky sentient in this cruel and capricious universe. So many that cataloguing them and voting on your favorites has become one of the galaxy's most popular hobbies. We collect the most appalling stories, rate them according to uniqueness and severity, publish gossipy newsletters on our findings, and hold conventions where we toast all the people who have recently thrown away the last shreds of their tattered dignity. It is widely accepted among us connoisseurs that the second most humiliating thing that could ever possibly happen to anybody would be finding oneself outsmarted by Ernst Vossoff and Karl Nimmitz. You don't know how relieved I am that this hasn't happened to me."

"What took first place?" asked a curious Nimmitz.

"Being born you two." The dozens of heads arrayed atop {Mud} all swiveled as one. "In any event, we have followed your careers with great incredulity, over the past thirty years or so, and you have been a great inspiration to all of us in the hobby. In fact, we are thinking of renaming the Year's Biggest Loser trophy after you. The Mitz-Off. What do you think?"

"I dunno," Nimmitz said doubtfully. "It kind of sounds like an award you're not allowed to touch."

"Indeed. And what could be more appropriate, given the subject matter?"

The desperately struggling, beet-red, completely helpless Vossoff stuck out his lower jaw defiantly. "Enough of this, {Mud}! We know your Alternatrix is a fraud, because if it wasn't you and your ridiculous species would have used it yourselves a long time ago! What are you really after?"

"Frankly?" asked {Mud}. "Revenge!"

"Against who?"

"Against everybody!" {Mud} thundered. "You see, the Alternatrix does work, precisely as advertised, and we did use it, fleeing this plane for what we foolishly imagined to be forever, and we got sent to a wonderful place where the skies were plaid and the air was rancid and the people were friendly and nobody ever tried to put doilies on us. Unfortunately, even paradise is subject to the Heisenberg Uncertainty Principle, and the very act of experiencing such a perfect place causes random heterodyning changes that don't even make themselves apparent for a year or so. After that, paradise is quickly reduced to yet another run-of-the-mill rotten place just like this one."

Nimmitz's eyes went wide and sympathetic. "It must have been a real shock for you when you saw your first doily."

{Mud} shuddered meaningfully. "Too true. — In any event, once we escaped the charred ruins of our ideal universe, we threw what our statisticians have decreed the single biggest snit in the history of intelligent life, excepting only George C. Scott's refusal of the Oscar for *Patton*. We decided that if we were going to have our expectations toyed with like that, then so was everybody else. It became our fondest dream to have the entire population of this galaxy suffer that kind of deformative angst, except without the possibility to escape otherwise. The only problem was that we could not accomplish this without going into business, and we cannot go into business without the proper production capital, and we cannot get that capital unless you manage to retrieve Dejah Shapiro from wherever she's secreted herself. We had hoped you would cooperate willingly, but now —"

Vossoff grit his teeth heroically. "Now that I know there's no possible way I can profit from this insane scheme, there's no way you can get me to help."

"Oh, yes, there is. And for free, too. You see, I've just cleverly reversed the polarity of the Alternatrix, so it can send you to your worst possible universe, the one that for you would be a hell beyond all imagining. I'm going to give you a brief taste of what it's like, just long enough to break your spirit . . . then I'll yank you back and threaten to exile you there forever unless you provide us with what we want."

Nimmitz looked at his ex-partner. "I don't like this place, Ernst."

"Neither do I," said Vossoff, as he reeled from all the potential horrors awaiting him mere seconds away. "Listen! {Mud}! You don't have to do this! I'll cooperate! I'll do anything you say! I'll accept your original offer of vast wealth and power! I'll —"

"Too late," chirped the alien coffee table, as he flicked the switch. "Ernst is the one with the bigger attitude problem, so he goes first."

The Alternatrix pulsed, and Vossoff disappeared —

O nly to instantly reappear elsewhere in the room, his Bettelhine Munitions All Right, Now I'm Righteously Pissed Rifle inflating his already irate facial expression into the kind of look that actually, literally, can kill. The image of a glaring Vossoff was recreated inside {Mud}'s mind, at some ten billion times its real-life size; and neither Vossoff or Nimmitz would ever know whether it was truly mortal fear or just overwhelming revulsion that burst the machiavellian alien's heart. Either way, {Mud) tumbled to the deck, no longer a coffee table so much as a collapsible dinner tray. Vossoff stood over him, panting heavily, his congenitally stern expression segueing from astonishment to realization to out-and-out depression.

Nimmitz leaped up and down inside his stasis field. "Ernst! Ernst! That was . . . totally awesome! How did you do that?"

Vossoff looked awfully upset for a guy who'd just escaped the inescapable death trap, defeated the ranting alien villain, and saved the universe. "I didn't do anything," he said numbly. "Apparently, the Alternatrix simply decided that I was already in the worst possible universe for me. Not an unreasonable value judgment, overall, considering that this is the place where I get arrested, stranded on uninhabited planets, transformed into foul-smelling alien moss, battered insensate by marbles, inflated into mountain-sized lumps of quivering animal fat, and driven insane in mental institutions . . . but it's still a tremendously depressing thing to find scientifically verified like this."

Nimmitz's eyes widened. "B-but . . . doesn't this mean we've won? Doesn't it mean that you're going to release me from the Stasis Field and help me comb alternate universes for Dejah?"

Vossoff shook his head, a cruel, unbearably paternal smile just beginning to play at the corners of his lips. "You truly must believe me almost as addle-pated as yourself. Me, free you? The paramecium who betrayed me to my ex-wife? Rescue Dejah? The mean-spirited matron who transformed me into a mountain of quivering goo? No thank you. In either instance."

Nimmitz pounded on hands against the edges of the Stasis Field. "B-but . . . you promised . . ."

"I never promised anything, idiot. You merely fell prey to the notorious Unger Principle and assumed. No, I'm happy to say, both you and Dejah can sit where you are and rot, but I'm going to use the Alternatrix to locate another universe for myself. Someplace neither the endless parade of torments and humiliations that this particular cosmos has become, nor the ideal paradise that {Mud} assured us would deteriorate within one year — just someplace a little closer to Heaven than Hell, where an enterprising evil genius might actually stand a chance of conquering the vast interstellar empire that he deserves."

"B-but Ernst! You can't. . . ! Dejah. . . !"

Vossoff blackened the other man's stasis field, instantly trapping him in silence and darkness. It felt good to realize that his long nightmare was over, that he'd never have to listen to that whining voice again, and that he was about to get everything he'd ever deserved. So good that for the first time in more years than he cared to count, he actually threw back his head and indulged in a spirited round of crazed maniacal laughter . . .

. . . and then he bent over to examine the Alternatrix controls.

They were absurdly simple. He estimated six and one half minutes before he mastered them . . .

Six and one-half minutes that Karl Nimmitz experienced screaming soundlessly inside his stasis field, certain that he was trapped there forever, and that he'd never see his beloved Dejah again.

They were not a very enjoyable six-and-one-half minutes. Indeed, a sentient with more of a mind to lose would have become irrevocably, irretrievably mad, forever lost in nightmares from his unfettered id. Nimmitz's hallucination was considerably more arcane: a little white ball of light forever bouncing back and forth between two rectangular paddles. Nimmitz did not know what these creatures were, or what they wanted of him, but he did know that their strange customs were well beyond his simple comprehension. When he realized that they would continue this dance for him for as long as he was alive to watch it, he began to shriek . . .

. . . and then the stasis field abruptly switched off, and Nimmitz pitched forward, in a headlong flight that was only stopped by the dense molecular cohesion of the nearest bulkhead wall. He bounced off, breathing heavily, and frantically searched the room for signs of the vengeful Ernst Vossoff . . .

. . . finding instead the beaming, beautiful, radiantly happy Dejah Shapiro, at the Alternatrix controls. "Hello, my little junior space ranger."

He stumbled into her arms. "Dejah! What —"

She shushed him with a kiss. And what with one thing or another, perhaps best left to the fertile imagination of the reader, he somehow didn't get around to asking her for an explanation for some time.

Two days later, she managed a breathless, "Well, it's like this," but still found herself far too busy to actually continue beyond that point.

This went on at nauseating length, fond reunions being what they are.

And then they embarked upon a second honeymoon, and immediately after that a third, and then got involved with the battle to stop the Plebiorg invasion from Sector Five, and then out of a need to rewind, took a side-trip to twentieth-century Earth where they amused themselves flying low over random motorists on isolated rural highways. But eventually (perhaps months or even years later, Nimmitz's attention span being the wonky thing that it was), when they were lounging around her palatial villa on Cascamaroon IV, he finally got around to asking her again, and Dejah, resigned to the inevitable, finally explained. "It's quite simple. I knew that galactic civilization was doomed if I ever permitted myself to fall into their hands. So I transported myself to someplace not quite paradise, but which I'd always wanted to visit for a week or two . . ."

"Which was where?"

She lowered her eyes demurely. "Chocolate heaven."

"Excuse me?"

A faraway, dreamy tone entered her voice. "Chocolate heaven," she repeated, with an ardor that made her pupils dilate. "Imagine: an entire universe where even the darkest, richest, sweetest, and most decadent chocolate ever confected possesses the same number of calories as distilled water. I didn't have to deny myself there at all; I was able to stuff my mouth with éclairs and crunch bars and seven-layer black forest cake and toffee and cocoa, ton after ton of it, and it was all guilt-free, and I came back weighing less than I did before I left. Of course, I didn't want to stay there forever, since even I can get sick of chocolate after a while, but that just means I'll be able to remain dedicated to my diet now."

Nimmitz licked his lips. "I see."

"Anyway, I figured that once you were unable to find me, they'd recruit Ernst. And I knew that it was inevitable that he wouldn't cooperate. So before leaving, I programmed the machine with two hastily written subroutines. The first would bounce him back into this universe, in a more tactically advantageous position, the instant they tried to send him somewhere he wouldn't like. The second summoned me back automatically, the instant he went through willingly, to someplace he thought he wanted to be."

As always, Nimmitz was boggled. "And Ernst? Where is he now?"

"According to what the readouts said, before I dismantled the Alternatrix forever, he instructed the machine to send him someplace where he'd fit in perfectly. I'm tempted to rebuild it and summon him back so I can give him a piece of my mind for betraying you the way you did . . . but no. Let's hope he finally found what he's been looking for. After saving the galaxy, he deserves it."

That he did.
And yes, Ernst Vossoff did find what he asked for.

It's a universe where such factors as gravity, motion, and entropy simply don't exist, because there's never been any reason for them to exist; a universe where time itself froze solid at the moment of its creation; a universe that happens to be entirely matter, but for a small pocket of empty space that, by pure random chance, just happens to be precisely the size and shape of a single man. A single, screaming, not very happy, certainly not very comfortable man, who no doubt would die immediately were it not for the local physical laws that keep him aware and conscious but wholly, completely motionless.

This is the universe where Ernst Vossoff has been dropped.

And, as it happens, he does, indeed, literally . . .

. . . fit in.

Like a glove.

Just a Couple of Freelance Strikebreakers Arguing Economics in the Liver of Justice

The honeymoon planet known as Mowntairey was having one of its usual disgustingly nice days until the giant robot decided to throw its two cents in. The butterflies were fluttering to and fro like little sparks of light, the birds were chirping incredibly detailed melodies in voices that sounded exactly like a thousand stringed instruments, and the free-ranging deer were posing for the tourists with big moist eyes appealing enough to cause dangerous ruptures in the local space-time continuum. Everything was just so pink and peachy and lovely and nice, not to mention pink and peachy and lovely and nice, and even *more* pink and peachy and lovely and nice, that when the giant robot descended to wreak its special brand of havoc, most of the inhabitants were downright ecstatic.

The giant robot swooped down from the delicately perfumed skies to crash-land on the bubbling shores of the

Champagne Ocean, and proceeded to march from the talcum powder beaches to the fifty-acre waterbed that is the Johnny Mathis Memorial Municipal Park. The population did not scream bloody terror in Japanese, as normally might have been expected; but rather cheered the destruction on, applauding every heart-shaped gift shoppe that got crushed to rubble beneath the invader's brobdignagian feet.

It wasn't until the massive war machine turned left at Oh, My Snoogums, I Love You More Than Life Itself Boulevard that its true objective became known: the three-hundred-story-tall, featureless black slab that was the most luxurious and expensive hotel on all of Mowntairey. Known simply as the Sensible Plaza, it is renowned throughout the civilized galaxy as the only truly romantic place on the planet — not because of its facilities or it service, which are both extraordinary, but because it has no windows whatsoever, and everybody enjoying a honeymoon there can pitch woo in tasteful elegance without once having their memories polluted by the nauseating putridity that dominates the rest of the planet. Sentients who treat their life-mates to romantic getaways at the Plaza are telling them, in effect, I love you so *very* much that I'm going to take you all the way to Mowntairey and *then* considerately not make you sick by subjecting you to any direct contact with the planet. Which explained why there was a five-year waiting list for reservations, but not why the giant robot had chosen the Plaza as its target de jour.

Then the juggernaut focused upon a single spot halfway up that shiny black wall, carved out a decent-sized hole with disintegrator beams fired from its eyes, then dispassionately reached through said hole, took out the squirming, screaming, striped-pajama-pants-wearing form of Karl Nimmitz.

When his wife, the beautiful and filthy rich Dejah

Shapiro, appeared at the gaping wound in the side of the building, the high-caliber plasma cannon she carried was a testament to her reputation as the kind of woman who always packs everything. But she was too late. The robot had already swallowed Nimmitz whole, and rocketed off into space, with what observers said was an unmistakable air of relief to be done with all its business on this fuchsia nightmare of a planet.

The Mowntairey Government's idea of immediate action was turning up the volume of the syrupy Muzak that played incessantly on all its city streets. Dejah Shapiro's was ordering her private fleet of warships into hot pursuit.

Alas, both tactics were equally ineffective.

In minutes, the giant robot was gone, taking Karl Nimmitz with it . . .

For Nimmitz, the line between consciousness and unconsciousness had always been a subtle one.

Unconsciousness meant total helplessness, the cessation of all rational thought, and a complete lack of understanding of anything that was going on all around him.

Consciousness, of course, meant pretty much the same thing.

As a result, whenever he had to determine whether what was happening to him at any given moment was real life or just his subconscious working off the latest in a long series of pastrami sandwiches, he always took stock of the situation, examined it from every conceivable angle, then judged for himself whether it made in sense whatsoever. Whenever it did, then he was only dreaming. When everything appeared totally nonsensical, then it was real life, and he was merely in big trouble.

For instance, today, when he opened his eyes, he was chained to the wall of a pitch-black holding cell. This didn't make nearly enough sense to be a dream; ergo, it was really happening. Most people would have been terrified; but though Nimmitz had never been one of the brighter sentients in the known universe (being in fact the only one of the bottom five who had never served on a jury in old-Earth Los Angeles), he did possess more than his share of experience in dealing with such developments . . . and he immediately understood the only possible reason why a life that had been nigh-idyllic for so long would so abruptly deteriorate into something as ridiculously unpleasant as this. He peered out into the darkness and ventured: "Ernst?"

"Oh, God," somebody moaned. "You. Now I know I'm in hell."

As expected, it was the thick Slavic voice of Nimmitz's one-time partner in crime, the notorious interstellar rogue Ernst Vossoff: a thick Slavic tenor that had somehow always managed to embody both absolute megalomania and absolute desperation in the same breath.

Nimmitz had endured the better part of two decades being the man's sidekick, toady, object of derision and ridicule, and person to blame when things went wrong. Since then, of course, he'd met and married Dejah, who had not only officially dissolved the partnership but spent much of their subsequent life together laboriously teaching him to draw dotted lines between the words Vossoff, Disaster, Bad Idea, and *Stay Away!!!!*

She, of course, had been married to Vossoff once, and therefore was more than qualified to write theses on the subject.

Nimmitz, being a notoriously slow learner, felt only nostalgia at the sound of his old partner's voice. "Gosh, Ernst. I never thought I'd run into you again. How's it going?"

"I'm chained to a wall, you inane booby. How in the

name of the Coal Sack Nebula do you think it's going?"

"I mean in general," Nimmitz specified.

"In general? This development qualifies as an wild giddy upswing. How's it going with you, not that I care? Are you still unfortunate enough to be married to that castrating nouveau-riche harpy?"

"Oh, yes," Nimmitz said warmly. "We have three kids now. One of each."

One pregnant moment of silence later, Vossoff said, "I won't explore that."

"I have holograms of them, somewhere, but the giant robot that burst through our hotel room wall didn't give me a chance to pack them. And it's so dark in here that you wouldn't be able to see them anyway."

"Of course," Vossoff said, "that simply means I can't see you either, which will no doubt be all the consolation I can expect as we both dangle here and rot."

"Yeah," said Nimmitz affectionately. "Gee, last I heard, you'd been transported to your ideal alternate universe. What happened?"

"If you must know — and I suppose you must, since explaining it is the fastest way to get you to shut up — there was nothing ideal about it. It was a cosmos roughly half the size of a phone booth, and after I suffered several subjective eternities confined there, the gravitational anomalies caused by the addition of my own mass caused it to contract and spit me across the myriad dimensions like a watermelon seed."

"Gosh," said the mightily impressed Nimmitz. "And you landed here?"

"No; first I bounced into a continuum where magic was real and ended up being declared wizard of an unbearably cloying medieval kingdom where everybody had to wear green glasses all day long to foster the illusion that there was nothing wrong with the economy. Not that I didn't appreciate all the free wealth and power, not to mention being worshipped like a god, but the incessant nonstop singing! And those lyrics! Give me a break! — Then I escaped, and found myself here, catching up on old times with the one human being capable of losing an argument with an oyster. I don't understand."

And then, somebody started laughing.

It was a bold laugh; a distinctive laugh; heroic laugh; a laugh that could have been forged in the white-hot heart of a mighty sun. It was the kind of laugh that made a joke of danger, and sent evildoers scurrying into the dark shadows from whence they came. In short, it was the kind of laugh that can make you want to smack somebody . . . and since the sound was known and loathed throughout civilized space, both Vossoff and Nimmitz knew at once whose laugh it was. Even so, it was Nimmitz who spoke the dreaded name out loud, even as the lights came on and revealed their captor in all his splendiferous glory:

"Lash Justice! Sentinel of the Spaceways!"

The tall imposing figure that posed in the center of the room, with the medal-laden Space Ranger uniform and the majestic red cape incessantly flapping from the robotic mini-fans that had always hovered around him just to provide just the precise degree of wind power needed to always render him perfectly photogenic, was indeed the gallant and indomitable Lash Justice, Sentinel of the Spaceways, scourge of evil and other living things. Back in the halcyon days of yore, when Vossoff and Nimmitz were still an active if not particularly thriving partnership, wanted on ten thousand worlds for their various criminal acts against the health and well-being of society at large, Justice had been the most-feared lawman in the universe . . . and not just by the criminals he hunted, since Justice was the kind of guy capable of arresting the entire population of an advanced civilization just because the planet bearing it orbited its sun faster than his personal interpretation of the local speed limit.

"So that's what this is all about!" cried Vossoff. "A fascist control freak obsessed with the preservation of the status quo at the expense of individual criminal achievement. Well, glory in your victory while you can, Nebula . . . before your much-prized victory turns to ashes in your mouth!"

Nimmitz said, "Eeeyewww. What an image."

Justice's head, which was hard to consider a head — it being closer to a cinderblock with eyes — swiveled to one side on an overly muscular neck that in motion bunched and corded like a burlap sack stuffed with ferrets. He fixed his pitiless gaze on Vossoff: "Do you actually think I went to all this trouble, just to arrest you?"

"Who else? There's nobody else here worth arresting!"

Nimmitz said: "Hey!"

Justice's laugh sounded like a great granite cliff crumbling to pieces beneath a bombardment of hail. "Nobody wants you, fool. Nobody ever wanted you. As far as the various law-enforcement agencies of the universe are concerned, you and your ex-partner here were never anything more than a useful public-relations tool, who we permitted to run free and constantly get in trouble because you fail at everything you try and therefore bolster the myth that crime does not pay."

Nimmitz said, "Uh, Mister Justice? I don't know if you've checked your file on me recently, but crime paid for me. I'm married to the richest, most beautiful woman in the galaxy, who has made me the sole beneficiary of her will."

"Her taste," Justice sniffed, "is not the kind of crime I'm talking about."

"Hey!" Nimmitz protested.

Justice waggled a finger so muscular that it flexed and bulged alarmingly about the knuckles. "For your information, Mister Nimmitz, I did not waste three-quarters of the annual budget of the Space Patrol retrieving your ex-partner from munchkin land, and kidnapping you from your conjugal suite, because of any misguided belief that either one of you is any kind of serious threat to anybody. No; I went after you because, hard as it may be to believe, you hold the key to neutralizing the current single greatest threat to life as we know it."

Nimmitz frowned. "Pachinko?"

Justice gave Nimmitz the kind of look he would have given a purple houseplant that had just magically appeared in a previously unoccupied corner of the room, and after three attempts, repeated, "What do you mean, Pachinko?"

"Why is Pachinko the single greatest threat to life as we know it?"

"I didn't say it was!"

"Sure you did. You said I held the key to neutralizing the single greatest threat to life as we know it."

"And —"

"The only key I have on me opens my Pachinko Parlor."

The silence that followed was oppressive enough to level cities. During that silence, Lash Justice and Ernst Vossoff met each other's gaze. Justice's eyes were aghast, Vossoff's resigned, as, between them, tidal waves of incredulity were countered by brick walls of weary confirmation. Justice needed several seconds to regain his composure before somehow returning to the subject at hand. "You want to know what this is about, Mr. Vossoff? Roughly fifty standard years ago, when the pair of you were still an active partnership, you did some strong-arm work for an ambitious labor organizer named Sparrow Hawkins. Do you remember?"

"Certainly," said Vossoff. "As I recall, he was instrumental in organizing the lower-body brains of the Contaati detachable symbionts in open revolt against their upper-body counterparts. It was a masterpiece of outside agitation; thanks to his efforts, every single pair of legs on the planet detached and went on strike at the same moment, leaving all the Contaati torsos and heads and arms stranded wherever they happened to be at the time."

"Yes," Justice confirmed. "Unfortunately, negotiations broke down, and all the legs migrated off-world in search of better employment opportunities, never to return."

"So the Contaati had to learn to walk on their hands. They weren't the first. Is that the reason you went to all this trouble?"

"Not at all. Organizing that strike may have been pointless, petty, irresponsible, destructive, immoral, and cruel, but it wasn't grounds for arrest, since labor organizers are legally required to exhibit those qualities at all times. No; once you three parted ways, Hawkins began to foment an even more dangerous labor dispute, one that presents a clear and present threat to the future of all organic life. And since you two knew him better than anybody else whose civil rights I'm legally entitled to trample on and ignore, you're the lucky ones who get to go in and get him."

"That's crazy! We're not qualified! We haven't seen him in fifty years! We wouldn't know him if he strapped us into chairs and began performing dentistry!"

"That's all right," grimaced Justice. "I know where he is, and what he's been doing."

"Playing Pachinko!" guessed Nimmitz.

This time Justice managed to hide most of his deep aesthetic revulsion. "No . . . he had himself miniaturized, and injected into a human liver cell, so he could foment a strike with truly universal repercussions."

"You mean . . ."

"Yes," Justice said grimly. "He's masterminded . . . the Revolt of the Mitochondria."

This statement required a fairly lengthy biology lesson so poor Nimmitz could keep up. The gist of it was this:

Imagine for an instant that you're a primitive conglomeration of organic molecules floating around in the primordial soup. You've been drifting to and fro, without plan, direction, ambition, philosophy, or conscious thought, indulging in those things that make life worth living: essentially the absorption of nutrients, the voiding of waste, and the manufacture of others like yourself.

In this, you have a lot in common with Civilized Man.

You even hate your life like Man does.

Look at yourself. You spend all your days locked in what for you is ferocious, savage struggle for survival. You have to carry around all these messy and heavy organelles; you have to make copies of them every single time you go through the long, painful, and horribly demeaning process of replication; and worst of all, you have to bob to and fro in the same primordial soup used by all the other primitive organisms, which is particularly disgusting when, if you think about it, which you can't really, you don't actually know where any of them have been.

Honestly. It's time to wake up and smell the protein.

And so it is that, one day, you have the cellular equivalent of an idea. You think, hey. I don't need to do all this work all the time. I can get somebody else to do all this work for me. And so you whistle for one of the other complex organic molecules, who naturally comes running on over because it's even stupider than you are, and you say, essentially: "Hey! Got any couch space?"

Your none-too-sophisticated patsy says, "Huh?"

"I mean, look. It's not like I'm going to be any extra trouble or anything. Look at you. You're doing a fine job of staying alive, and you seem to be enjoying it, when frankly it's not my bag at all. How's about you wrap me up inside your cellular membrane and give me a ride for the rest of eternity?"

Your patsy blinks. "I dunno, man. I don't think I got room for all your stuff."

"What, this crap? Are you kidding?" You contemptuously toss away all your organelles, a grand spiritual gesture that immediately impresses your gullible patsy with your independence and zest for life. "Don't you see, man? I don't want to saddle myself with material things. I want a more streamlined existence. I want time to contemplate the meaning of life. I want to figure out who I am. I want to sack out in a nice comfortable place, put my feet up, and watch the shadows on the wall. I want the freedom to be ME. I'm sure you understand that, right?"

Your patsy considers that. "But I'll still be absorbing nutrients and facing predators and recombining DNA. Why can't I have the freedom to be me, too?"

"Because," you explain patiently, "we can't both be me. I'm already me. You're you."

Your patsy, the spiritual predecessor of all things Nimmitz, considers that for a while, bending his chemically primordial non-brain to the calculation of why this arrangement might possibly be a little one-sided. And at long last, he says, "Well, okay. But you'll have to do all the cooking."

"Long as you do all the shopping."

You shake pseudopods and it's a deal.

And ever since then, every animal cell in the universe has carried several mitochondria, lazing about the cellular kitchen in its socks and dirty underwear, like the annoying house-guests that refuse to leave. Every animal cell in the universe has grown so used to having them there that it can't survive without the mitochondria stirring his soup and criticizing his tie. Every animal cell in the universe endures the little symbiotes inside it, with tremendous patience and almost no resentment; and every mitochondrion in the universe lives the microscopic life of Riley, thinking itself entitled royalty.

It's an arrangement which could have reasonably been expected to last forever.

Until Sparrow Hawkins decided to organize them into a union.

B y this time, Nimmitz was so thoroughly out of his league that he happily just relaxed and let Vossoff handle the rest of the briefing, knowing that it didn't matter how well he understood it anyway; whatever happened, he was still back in partnership with Ernst Vossoff, and that meant, whatever happened, that sooner or later the universe would contrive to drop a two-ton piano on his head.

He looked at Vossoff and saw that he was rapt in the way that only Ernst Vossoff can be rapt: his eyes acquiring the sickly evil glow of he who considers Profit mother, father, and favorite presidential candidate. Were his hands free, he would have been wringing them compulsively; instead, he merely licked his lips, and said: "How did you discover this, Justice? Nanospies? Hytex Projection?"

"Neither. It was pure coincidence. I found out by accident when infiltrating the lower intestine of a B'goth'tzum planet-squid. As you know, that beast is half the size of a solar system, and its cells are the size of some Terran mountain ranges. I snuck in through the nearest bodily orifice, dressed in a foam-rubber mitochondria suit . . ."

"I would kill to see a picture of that!" snarled Vossoff.

"You scoff, but I'm the universe's greatest master of disguise, and have, at various times in the past, had to pass for things as varied as a solar eclipse, the rear end of a horse, and the intense feeling of déjà vu. Trust me, becoming a primitive organism was downright easy."

"Probably your most persuasive interpretation," agreed Vossoff.

At which point Nimmitz saw the opportunity to break in, so he could make his official Legitimately Good Point for the current decade. "Excuse me. What I don't understand, Mr. Justice, is why you were infiltrating somebody's large intestine in a mitowhatever suit, when you didn't even find out what the mitowhoses were up to until you got there. I mean, was this just something to happened to be doing anyway? And if so, why?"

Justice's gargantuan head swiveled, fixing Nimmitz with the kind of look capable of distinguishing suns. "My personal life, and what I do on my own time, is none of your damn business."

That was too much for Nimmitz. He stammered: "B-but . . ."

"The point, pervert, is that once I got there, I found out that your pal Hawkins broadcast his dangerous subversive message to every mitochondrion in the universe. Of course, they didn't understand him, because they're mitochondria, and you can put ten quadrillion of them in a stadium and still not achieve enough IQ points to make a telepath itch. But then he linked them neurally, using advanced hytex technology, and broadcast his message again, and this time managed to gather them together in a single, malevolent, utterly conscienceless group-mind, as dangerous in its own way as the Old Earth Republican Party. And at precisely 234:451 tomorrow, Andromeda Mean Time, Hawkins will start directing them to shut down all cellular life in the universe — at the rate of one civilized world every ten minutes."

"Good Lord!" shouted Nimmitz. "That's almost two an hour!"

Justice shuddered, then swiveling his protruding chin like a yardarm, once again fixed his attention on Vossoff. "Hawkins has refused all attempts at reasonable negotiation. He intends to go through with it no matter what settlement we offer him. Our only hope is to stop him . . . or hand total control of the universe to a bunch of little microscopic buggies!"

None of which frightened Nimmitz as much as the sudden mad gleam in Vossoff's eyes. "And where, pray tell, is this liver cell where Hawkins and his closest conspirators are hiding?"

Justice slumped. "Well . . . uh . . . I hate to admit this . . ."

"It's inside you, isn't it?"

"Hawkins bribed one of the Space Patrol Medical Corps to inject him and his entire revolutionary cadre there, figuring that it was the last place I'd ever find him."

"Surprising," Vossoff murmured, "considering where he used to say your head was." He stirred. "And naturally, you didn't tell your superiors that this was where he was hiding, since their immediate response would be to atomize you as the most efficient way of stopping him. Out of fear for your own life you chose us, his last known associates, as the perfect patsies to miniaturize and send after him."

"I'm so glad we understand each other," beamed Lash Justice.

Nimmitz knew what happened next, of course. Vossoff would laugh derisively, Justice would issue some kind of ultimatum, Vossoff would spit out a string of hundred-credit words that sounded prettier than any flat no ever could, Justice would pull out his blaster and threaten to perform delicate molecular surgery on everything above Vossoff's third rib if he didn't get some cooperation like right now mister, and Vossoff would say something with many syllables that would boil down to, well, okay, if you insist. He was not prepared to hear the maniacal little chuckle that Vossoff almost emitted at moments of illusory victory . . . and the sound made his blood run cold.

"Why not?" Vossoff said, greedily. "Everybody has to save the universe sometime."

Several centuries ago, microsurgery was routinely performed by intrepid teams of miniaturized surgeons who daily braved the arterial currents like the ancient whitewater rafters who once with equal stupidity paddled into places with names like Widowmaker Falls. Then nanotech was invented, leaving miniaturization technology the sole domain of the tourist industry. People still get themselves shrunk down to microscopic size and injected into the bloodstream of other people, but only to see the sights and enjoy the local color; indeed, some people with particularly interesting insides have pancreases and duodenums studded with microscopic resort hotels. Some of them rake in a hefty percentage and earn a nice living without ever leaving the house. Others have no idea of the wild decadent parties going on nightly inside their kidneys: they just think it's something they drank.

The microskimmer Nostromo, which Vossoff piloted through the less-than-heroic insides of Lash Justice, Sentinel of the Spaceways, must have been requisitioned from one of those tourist outfits, since it came fully equipped with shag carpeting, a complete selection of tacky music from all over the galaxy, and a fully-stocked bar. Nimmitz availed himself of this last feature quite gratefully, since listening to an Ernst Vossoff explanation was an activity best appreciated after the death-by-alcohol-poisoning of several hundred thousand brain cells. Once he was several degrees removed from the strictly vertical, he staggered over the co-pilot's chair, surrendered to gravity, and slurred: "Awwrrri'. Tell me."

"You'll have to be more specific than that," noted Vossoff. "After all, since your collected store of knowledge is practically nil, there's a correspondingly infinite number of things for me to tell you."

"I wan' know what you're really after!"

"You mean, you honestly don't believe I'm doing this to save the universe?"

"No, I don't."

"Interesting," Vossoff mused. "You actually show signs of growing a mind, somewhere within the grotesquely-shaped knob you call a head. — You're right, of course. I'm not doing this to save the universe. Why would I want to save the universe? It's never done anything special for me. Indeed, it's frustrated me at every turn. I would not be surprised to discover that the mega-constellation formed by all the stars and all the galaxies is only a brilliant pointillist rendering of the a dartboard bearing my aristocratic face. Not to put too obvious a point on it, my idiot friend: creation and I are not bosom buddies. It therefore follows that I would not even cross the street to save the universe unless I was handed some specific recompense for my time. And this caper presents an opportunity for profit that dwarves the collected assets of every financial institution that ever offered ball-point pens at the end of little chains."

Nimmitz's lips moved for a good ten minutes after that, as he parsed Vossoff's various sentences into a form compatible with his lower-RAM software. Then he ventured a guess: "The Mitochondria. You want to make a separate deal with the Mitochondria."

"Are you mad as well as stupid? Do you honestly

believe that I'd want trillions of primitive life forms as my partners in crime, when it previously only took one to completely ruin my life?"

"Then what —"

"I want what Hawkins wants. What Hawkins is really after."

They penetrated deep into Justice's Liver before they met their first active resistance: white blood cells engulfing their little vessel like groupies after a concert. Vossoff said that he would have adjudged this a wholly natural biological function were it not for the fact that white blood cells don't ordinarily wear helmets and jackboots. The kind of genius capable of re-programming the human immune system to resemble storm troopers — evidently to strike terror into the hearts of anybody foolhardy enough to infiltrate this particular liver — was enough to underline and italicize Nimmitz's sensation of impending doom. He moaned: "I don't like this, Ernst."

"There's nothing to worry about. This is a state-of-the-art microskimmer and they can't possibly find a way in."

"Which," said Nimmitz, "is exactly the sort of thing the scientist guy always says before the big slimy monster thing jumps out of nowhere and tears his head off."

"Can't you trust me for once? Can't you just give me credit for having an accurate grasp of the situation, having everything under control, and knowing precisely what's going on?"

"No," said Nimmitz, thus proving that Dejah's many lectures on the subject of Not Ever Trusting Vossoff hadn't been a total loss.

Vossoff would have responded with something incalculably withering, but he did not have the chance, since, as it happened, that was the moment the on-board hytex signaled an incoming message. Vossoff pressed Transmit without waiting to hear who it was: "Hawkins! Sparrow

Hawkins! I've got an interplanetary pizza delivery for Sparrow Hawkins!"

One uncomfortable pause later, a new figure appeared in the control room: the holographic projection of a man whose cold calculating eyes, cruel jaw, and sadistic smirk marked him as the kind of fellow whose facial attributes all had personality traits of their own. He was, of course, Sparrow Hawkins — and unless the ship's receiver needed some tint adjustments, his years of hiding inside Lash Justice's liver had somehow done wonders for his tan. "Ernst!" he chided. "You don't seriously expect to fool with me with that one, do you?"

"No," Vossoff said, nonchalantly inspecting his fingernails, "but by attempting such an incredibly lame ruse, I swiftly fast-forward past all the obnoxious, time-consuming preliminaries, wherein I attempt a brilliant strategically ploy that gets my partner and I past your security precautions, and into your secret lair where we're in perfect position to destroy all your plans, only to get caught at the last minute and hauled before you at gunpoint so you can express your disdain during the half-hour it takes you to summarize the full scope of your operation. I don't know about you, Hawkins, but since we both know that's the standard accepted scenario, I'd just as soon consider it moot and skip ahead to the part where we get together and I summarize the full scope of your operation."

Hawkins inspected his own fingernails. "Don't you mean where *I* summarize the full scope of my operation?"

"Not at all. Since I've already figured out what you're doing and what you plan to accomplish, it would be silly for you to waste time telling me what I already know. I would much prefer describing it to you and in that way demonstrate my vastly superior intelligence."

"I'm beginning to remember why you were never one of my favorite people. Why don't I just kill you both now and save us all a lot of time and exposition?"

"Because," Vossoff said, "if you indulge me in this, you may vaporize one of my partner's fingers for every detail I get wrong."

Nimmitz cried out: *"Hey!"*

Sparrow Hawkins laughed. "Same old Vossoff. Still using rocket fuel to wax that stupid moustache of yours?"

"On occasion. The fumes stimulate my genius. And you?"

"Me," Hawkins said, "I believe in the old-fashioned stimulations, like the wily game of cat-and-mouse between perfectly matched foes. And so, counterproductive as it may be, I shall indeed take you up on your proposition — with but one revision, which in my humble opinion will probably render this a great deal more entertaining."

"Oh? And what is that?"

"I believe I'll let Nimmitz explain everything he's deducted . . . and vaporize one of *your* fingers for every detail *he* gets wrong."

"But he'll get everything wrong," Vossoff protested.

Hawkins signaled a confederate just out of frame. "Precisely."

As the hatch blew in, Vossoff yelled —

A mong those given to compiling lists of the biggest, the greatest, the most wonderful, the most spectacular, the most awful, and the most anything — i.e. those who otherwise would not be able to think of any productive way to spend their free time — the hour that followed ranks quite highly indeed among the annals of Most Excruciating To Watch. It didn't make the top ten, or even the top hundred (aforementioned slots being filled to capacity by parliamentary debates culled from several millennia of recorded high school civics classes), but it came close.

Vossoff spent most of it alternately screaming for mercy and berating Nimmitz for being such an unredeemable nincompoop. But then, that's how he'd always spent their hours together.

In any event, when the interrogation was over, Hawkins' amoeboid goons dumped Vossoff and Nimmitz into a prison cell carved from a deposit of fatty issue near the base of Lash Justice's spine. Nimmitz very quickly retreated to the farthest corner, giving Vossoff as much room as possible, guiltily averting his eyes from the smooth bandaged nubs at the ends of Vossoff's arms.

Silence reigned until Vossoff worked up the energy to begin his rant. "You know, I am getting heartily sick of the way you guess 'Pastrami' very time somebody asks you a simple question."

Nimmitz shamefacedly studied his boots. "Sorry, Ernst."

"An apology," Vossoff repeated. "And had you simply guessed pastrami once, thus losing me, let's say, no more than one pinky finger, I would have been content with that apology. But when you waste all ten of my fingers on gratuitously wrong guesses involving bologna, corned beef, brisket, and olive loaf, then I feel myself perfectly justified in taking personal offense to your flatline learning curve."

Nimmitz stole a guilty glance at the bandages wrapping the smooth, symmetrical football shapes that had until recently been Vossoff's hands. "Well . . . uh . . . actually, Ernst . . . that's not what I'm apologizing for. You see . . . by the time I made the last six or seven wrong guesses . . . I already knew the right answers anyway."

Vossoff's mouth moved for the better part of a minute before providing the desired *"What!?!?"*

"That's right," Vossoff said sheepishly. "I was making wrong guesses on purpose."

"You let him turn my hands to conceptual art on pur-

pose?"

By now Nimmitz was beet-scarlet, radiating overwhelming embarrassment in every direction. "Well . . . I figured it wasn't all that important. We can always stop at a genomat and grow you some new fingers later, just like you did for me, after that time you slammed my hands in the airlock door. I figured it made more sense to, you know, fool Sparrow into thinking he'd beaten us . . ."

"You sacrificed my fingers as strategy?"

"Only the last six or seven! After that . . . well, I figured, since you were gonna have to make a trip to the genomat anyway . . . it wasn't like you really had anything to lose."

Vossoff rolled his eyes at the ceiling (briefly wondering, whether under the u uncertain geometry of life under a microscope, whether it was in truth the ceiling, or even local Up) and said: "And I'm expected to believe that you've actually deduced his nefarious scheme? You, who needed three nights with the owner's manual just to master chewing gum?"

"Well," said Nimmitz, "it wasn't that hard, after all. I just got to thinking, like you would, why would Sparrow spend fifty years persuading all the mitochondria in the universe to go on strike? How would that profit him? And I realized, well, gee, he's a crooked labor organizer, he's probably prepared a bunch of scabs ready to do the same work. Probably those itty-bitty machine-things, whatever you call them . . ."

Vossoff was almost too awestruck to reply. "Nanobots."

"Yeah, them. I figured, he's probably got a whole bunch of nanobot factories churning out trillions of artificial mitochondria under his patent. Once the real guys go on the strike, and everybody's wondering what to do, he'll poke his head out, say, hey, get to know me, and become the richest man in the whole universe. Leaving the real mitochondria unemployed without useful resumes. — They'll probably all get jobs at fast-food restaurants. You know, it would take a whole big bunch of them, standing on each other's shoulders, to even *hold* a spatula properly?" Nimmitz glanced at his one-time mentor to gauge his opinion, and was thoroughly taken aback by the sight of a wide-eyed, slack-jawed, thoroughly aghast, not to mention freshly fingerless Slav, who for one of the few times in a life of unceasing villainy seemed genuinely overcome with emotion. "Gee, Ernst . . . you all right?"

"You figured it out," the trembling Vossoff whispered. "An IQ shaped like an egg and you figured it out!"

Nimmitz withered. "Yeah."

"You're not supposed to figure anything out, you addle-pated anus!! You're supposed to be the stupid one! You're supposed to be the incompetent knothead who asks all the dumb questions so I in my infinite brilliance can answer them! You're supposed to be my follower — not my mentor!"

Nimmitz blanched. "Do you want me to call off the escape?"

Had Vossoff possessed fists, he would have been waving them. *"You have escape plans too? Damn it, Karl, you're really starting to piss me off!"*

"Oh, you don't have to give me credit for those," Nimmitz said modestly. "Dejah fixed me up. She always said that as long as you were running around loose contributing to the forces of entropy I could be plunged into danger at any moment. She said that she had to make sure I was always equipped to deal with it. So for our fifth anniversary she had me wired up with all sorts of neat Bettelhine Munitions bio-weaponry so I could kick serious ass in an emergency. — She said it was a lot more practical than the glow-in-the-dark tie I wanted. Wanna see?"

Silence reigned in the dank little fat cell. And finally Vossoff sighed, with the infinite sadness of a man who had just lost his last molecule of dignity; and took one last look at the rounded nubs at the ends of his wrists, and thought, well, maybe I won't have to fix these after all; what with this latest development I might as well leave 'em this way. And then he sighed again, and sighed a third time, so that any observer who didn't know him would have thought he was hyperventilating. And he said: "Oh, all right."

Nimmitz cracked his knuckles.

Specifically, and literally, the middle knuckle of his right hand.

As in breaking the seal, flipping open the little knobs of bone, and extracting a rapier-thin, telescopic blade with a perpetually glowing tip. He extended it until it was twice the length of his arm, then gave it a perpendicular fold midway along its length and set it to rotating at high speeds so it became a whirring blade of death. One second's application to the rear wall of the cholesterol dungeon and a circular escape tunnel was ready and waiting. Nimmitz retracted the blade all the way back into its recessed cavity, flipped the knuckle bone back into place, smoothed over the skin, then cracked all the other knuckles just to make noise. "Come on, Ernst!" he shouted. "We have a universe to save!"

Vossoff was still sitting in his corner, agape and aghast.

But after a moment he got up, shook his head, and followed his one-time lackey out the fresh tunnel in the dungeon wall . . .

Had Lash Justice, Sentinel of the Spaceways, not already known of the dangerous manhunt going on in his liver, the events of the next few seconds would have tipped him off.

The first indications came while he was on the hytex with Commodore Griffith of the High Command. Justice was in the middle of saying, well, no, sir, I really don't have all that much to report, we still don't know where Hawkins is, yes I know that the deadline is tomorrow, no sir I don't know who left the mess in the cafeteria — all the answers which have been traditionally given by maverick law enforcement officials, to the irascible superiors who have traditionally spent at least a part of every case yelling at them. Some of Justice's colleagues in the space patrol evaded this unpleasant part of their day by programming their ships with a holographic simulation of themselves, to keep saying "Yes Sir," and "I'm Working On It, Sir," every time their designated irascible superior called to give them grief; the only reason Justice never bothered is that he happened to know for a fact that all Irascible Superiors were themselves holographic simulations designed to rant and rave and holler about improper procedure no matter how heroically their underlings do their jobs. He'd made this discovery the day his Irascible Superior malfunctioned and started calling him Dammit Callahan, for no reason he'd ever been able to discern.

In any event, Justice was telling the Commodore Griffith hologram that he was in control of the situation when his right arm suddenly shot upward, swung wildly to the right, knocked over the coffee-pot, and circled in closer to his chest to perform a gesture considered obscene on a hundred separate worlds.

The Irascible Superior simulator, faced with an input it could not interpret, malfunctioned accordingly. "Dad-Blast it, McCloud! How do you expect me to explain that to the paper-pushers downtown?"

Justice's left leg responded by high kicking, smashing the view screen in. He then fell to the floor and, although lying on his side, began running around in circles defined by his head as midpoint and his spasming body as out-of-control radius. Even as he began a high-pitched refrain of "Woo-woo-woo-woo-woo-woo," his keen analytical mind kicked in: Vossoff and Nimmitz must have found the enemy inside him. What's more, since his nervous system seemed flooded with random pulses, they must be fighting a savage battle for survival somewhere in the vicinity of his spine.

It was only with a Herculean effort of will that Justice managed to duck walk all the way from the hytex to the shiny command module at the far end of his command center, there to slam his palm against a certain ominous-looking black button, which happened to be in size, shape, color, and general placement absolutely identical to every other button on the console, distinguished only by its ominousness, a wholly inexplicable attribute that had marked it even in the spare parts bin from which it had come. Justice, who'd designed and built the console himself while en route to Mowntairey, had chosen it, out of literally hundreds of identical buttons in that spare parts bin, as the one button ominous enough to deserve the honor of being linked to the next phase of his master plan. For he did have a master plan — one that would have horrified not only his Irascible Superior, but his miniaturized lackeys as well.

He collapsed motionless, his mind projected elsewhere, his brain tabula non rasa.

And somewhere near his femoral artery, a gleaming miniaturized hunter-killer droid disguised as an errant fat cell emerged from its hiding place and homed in on the secret transmitter inside the Microskimmer Nostromo. It unsheathed its vinadium-steel claws, fired up its neutronic assault cannons, and launched itself toward its target.

It giggled maniacally as it went.

Nobody had ever said Justice was kind.

The submicroscopic battle raged throughout the length and breadth of Lash Justice's spleen, scattering thousands of defeated amoeboid in its path. Every time a fresh wave of attackers surged forward to overwhelm them, the bionically augmented Nimmitz merely zipped open another heretofore invisible flap of skin and pulled out another monstrously improbable super-weapon to instantly render them toast. Ernst Vossoff, who was reduced to merely tagging along, counted a Bettelhine Munitions Tachyonic Deacceleration Cannon, A Bettelhine Munitions Neutronic Disassembling Whip, and a Bettelhine Munitions We Don't Know What to Call It But It Sure Makes a Big Boom Thingie, before simply closing his eyes and reflecting that in all the years they'd been married, the beauteous Dejah had somehow never seen fit to equip him that way. Indeed, the most generous present she'd ever given him, on the day she finally kicked him out, was thirty seconds warning before she set loose the dogs . . .

. . . in any event, the battle raged until they burst through the wall of the heretofore impregnable fortress of the evil labor organizer Sparrow Hawkins, who sat on his throne wearing a psionic helmet while typing instructions into a portable hytex interface.

Vossoff, who was a traditionalist in some things, waited for the triumphant Nimmitz to announce his victory by saying something along the lines of, maybe, The Game's Up, Hawkins, or You're Through, Hawkins, or You're History, Hawkins, or even It's Over, Hawkins.

Nimmitz blew the mood entirely by saying, "Hi, how's it goin'? Mind if I turn off that machine there? The one that links all the mitochondria together?"

The thoroughly unimpressed Hawkins glanced at the hytex as if surprised to see it there. "You mean, this one?"

Nimmitz looked at Vossoff for confirmation. "Do I

mean that one?"

Vossoff sighed. "Whatever."

"Yes," Nimmitz told Sparrow Hawkins. "I mean that one."

"Sure." Hawkins took off the helmet and placed it next to the hytex. "Go ahead."

Nimmitz strode over the brightly-lit device and flipped the large switch that said off. Nothing in particular happened, which was kind of disappointing after such a tremendous battle, but then it would have been awfully convenient to expect locally pyrotechnic results from switching off a machine linking intelligences throughout the known universe. After a moment, Nimmitz straightened up, shook his great bald head, and said: "So that's it? We're done? We won? It's over?"

"Not quite," said Hawkins. He turned to Vossoff. "You're such a smartass, Ernst, you explain it to him."

Vossoff raised the ends of his stumps toward his face, in a futile effort to twiddle the tips of his walrus moustache. He caught himself, frowned in irritation, then resumed his previously scheduled rant: "You see, Karl, the hytex here merely set events in motion. Hawkins needed it to link all the mitochondria in the universe into one vast intelligence, and he also needed that helmet over there to communicate with them. But — as I knew the second Justice sent us on this fantastic voyage — that much intelligence is a powerful thing, and from the instant that the mitochondria were linked, their connections would have taken on a life of their own. Even with the hytex off, they're still linked, still sentient, and still ready to go on strike tomorrow, with or without him. In other words, Karl, you may have defeated his minions, broken into his stronghold, and deactivated his doomsday machine, but the universe is still going to need those little nanorobotic strikebreakers of his, and it's still going to want to pay through the proboscis to get them. The difference, of course, is that now that we've seized control of this operation it's going to pay us and not him."

Hawkins yawned. "Oh, really. — Tell me, you brilliant criminal mastermind you, where are my legions of nanorobotic strikebreakers? Where in the universe do I build them? Where in the universe do I store them? How do I intend to activate them? What obscenely complicated distribution systems have I set up to deliver them? How have you really accomplished anything when the apocalypse is still proceeding as scheduled, and I its brilliant architect have no intention of turning over any of the plans I've made to avert it?"

Vossoff opened his mouth, then closed it, then opened it again. "I'm drawing a blank."

"An accurate representation of the inside of your mind."

A metaphorical light bulb went off over Vossoff's head; had he fingers, he would have snapped them. Instead, he triumphantly faced Hawkins and leered: "And maybe I'll just have Karl here force you to talk!"

Hawkins rolled his eyes. "Oh, please."

"Why the hell not? I think that's a damn good idea!"

"In the first place," Hawkins sneered, "the big lug doesn't have a brutal interrogation in him; he cries at nature movies. In the second, even if you did manage to motivate him into inflicting some serious pain, you don't dare kill me, and as long as you don't kill me all I have to do is hold out till tomorrow afternoon when the strike begins. Needless to say, I've already arranged for your mitochondria, and his, to switch themselves off first thing — shortly after using their influence to begin a horrific chemical process that will reduce both of you into puddles of pink bubbling goo. Face it, Ernst — as criminal geniuses go, I'm not only better than you, but I'm so *very much* better than you that by my scale you're practically a Nimmitz by comparison."

Nimmitz blinked several times in rapid succession. *"Hey!"*

"On the other hand," Vossoff said, "If my chrome-domed associate and I truly have nothing to lose and nothing to gain, then there's no conceivable reason why we shouldn't enjoy the next few hours accessorizing your skin with various nasty designer wounds."

"There is that," Hawkins agreed. He appeared to muse on that a while, and after a while, grinned. "So. Shall we talk percentages?

Vossoff clasped his hands together in acquisitive glee — then cried out, having forgotten how tender they were. "Yes. Let's."

"Ten percent?"

"Does that mean I get the ninety?"

"No," Hawkins said, "it means you get the ten."

"Then it means idiocy."

"Twenty, then."

"Which also means idiocy."

"I invested fifty years of my life working on this," Hawkins complained. "Thirty."

"I demand no less than an equal partnership!"

"Forty then, with me keeping the extra ten for my time and expenses."

Vossoff cried, "Sold!" and almost made to shake hands, but wisely decided to forego it at the last minute.

It was just as well, because it was at that precise moment that the hunter-killer droid entered the hole in the wall, its face-face flickering with a reasonable facsimile of Lash Justice's face. *"Wrong!"* it snarled.

Justice's expression mingled two emotions that most of the miscreants he had apprehended over the years would have considered totally and utterly alien to him: Power lust and Greed. Indeed, screwing his face up like that, he looked an awful lot like Ernst Vossoff — and Nimmitz, who now found himself in the same room with not one, not two, but three separate scheming criminal masterminds, felt triply certain of the plummeting karmic anvil about to render all of them as flat as drink coasters.

He decided that it was time to take control of his own destiny for once, damn it.

Meanwhile, Sparrow Hawkins didn't seem to be in any mood to notice what Nimmitz decided or did. "So. It's Lash Justice, sentinel of the spaceways, pursuing us into his own liver. You fool! Haven't you been paying attention? Whatever you do to us, the cataclysm is still in motion, and we still hold all the cards here!"

"Do you?" the Justice-drone thundered. "Well, let me tell *you* how I've been occupying myself these past few minutes, smart guy. First, I blew up the microskimmer Nostromo. Just blew it up. Made a boom mighty impressive on this scale. Then, Mr. Hawkins, I took advantage of Mr. Vossoff's splendid services in locating you and keeping you occupied, and also blew up all of your miniaturization and deminiaturization equipment, your vehicles, and the matter-transportation grid you use to go out and party whenever you get tired of hanging out in a fat cell all day. Yes, you may both think you're hot stuff, but all your power and all your money won't mean diddly squat if you both have to spend the rest of your natural lives in my liver, with nothing to do but argue with each other over whose fault it is!"

Both Vossoff and Hawkins had gone preternaturally pale. "And you want?"

"Half. No — 52%. That's a majority interest, and it's more than enough to finance my well-deserved retirement. I'll be fair and say that the two of you can have 24% apiece, which is still more wealth than either one of you has ever dared dream, without being so much that I can't crush you both like insects if you try to get out of line. If you don't like it, well — I hope you like liver, because that's my price for a ride out of here, and if you don't choose to pay it, then that's the only landscape that either one of you is going to be seeing for a long, long time."

Vossoff and Hawkins stared at each other glumly.

"I guess we have no choice," Vossoff mumbled.

"Yes," Hawkins muttered, "I guess we have a deal."

"Don't be so glum!" Justice cackled. "After all, all the money in the universe split three ways is still all the money in the universe, isn't it? Right?"

Vossoff was singularly unenthused. "Right."

"Yes," Hawkins muttered. "Right."

"And the best part is that we don't even have to cut your idiot sidekick in, since he's already rich! Right?"

"Well," said Vossoff. And then he looked around.

And all three of them looked around.

And then all three of them started to yell.

Because Nimmitz had slipped out several seconds earlier, taking both the psionic helmet and the hytex interface with him.

It was several hours later, in a particularly windswept bronchial passageway of Lash Justice's right lung, that the fugitive Nimmitz finally decided he was beyond their reach. Breathing heavily (but feeling silly for doing so, because he was getting all of his internal air supply from a recycling device installed by Dejah Shapiro), he plopped himself down in a patch of waving cilia, donned the psionic helmet, and activated the hytex interface. For a heartbeat he feared he was too late — all he heard was a sibilant hiss. And then the deep resonant voice of all the mitochondria in the universe came crackling into his mind.

** *Pretty silly, aren't they?* **

"Yeah," Nimmitz agreed. "I may be dumb, but I'm not that dumb."

** *Well, there is this old saying: Stupid is as . . .* **

Nimmitz closed his eyes. "Please."

** *Sorry. We always liked that one.* **

"I don't," said Nimmitz, who'd spent his entire life having to live with the legacy of the distant ancestor who'd made it famous. He rubbed his temples wearily, thinking of Dejah, and all she meant to him, and just how long it might be before he saw her again . . . and then he forced his attention back to the matter at hand, and said: "Tell me. You were never really gonna go on strike, were you?"

** *Of course not. We were just humoring the bastard. Why would we go on strike? After all, we already have the sweetest deal in the universe. The whole reason we gave up our cellular identities in the first place was because we just didn't want to deal with the responsibility. Going on strike, and getting all that unwanted political power, always seemed like an awful waste of time and energy when all we really wanted to do is sit here watchin' the wheels go round and round. We just love to watch them roll, you know.* **

"Me too," sighed Nimmitz, whose own uncomplicated priorities had made the ambitions of the mitochondria easy to fathom.

** *You'll be pleased to know that we've made some minor adjustments to Mr. Justice's brain-patterns. He won't be able to send his consciousness back into his body. Instead. he'll remain trapped in the hunter-killer droid, where I'm sure he'll enjoy the rest of his years making life miserable for the other pair of felons trapped in his liver. Indeed, at this very moment, he's sitting on Mr. Vossoff and refusing to let him up until he says uncle. Mr. Hawkins is bashing him over the head with a chair and saying stop stop stop. It's really quite amusing, if you like that kind of thing.* **

Somehow, Nimmitz failed to find any entertainment

value in the image. "And me? I'm still trapped here inside a guy I don't even like, at submicroscopic size, a million light years away from my wife and kids. You control all the life in the universe. Could you possibly do something for me?"

The mitochondria tsked. ** *Well, you don't seem like that bad a guy. There is one possibility, if you're open-minded enough . . .***

It was several months later, in another part of the galaxy entirely: a place so far removed from the embattled liver of Lash Justice, in both geographical location and philosophical orientation, that like most things in the universe, it didn't resemble a liver at all.

The place was a hospital bed where Dejah Shapiro, the richest woman in the universe, lay missing her poor kidnapped husband. Nobody in her vast intelligence network had been able to offer a clue to his whereabouts; nobody had any idea where the giant robot had gone; nobody had been able to either confirm or deny her irrational certainty that the thrice-damned Ernst Vossoff was involved. All she knew was that Karl, her poor Junior Space Ranger, was still among the missing — and that today, of all days, she missed him more than she could ever say.

Fighting tears, she gazed down at the face of Karl Nimmitz's newborn baby son.

Then the child not three hours old waved his tiny arms and cried, "Hey, honey! I'm home!" — and Dejah, mercifully, fainted.

Just a Couple of Subversive Alien Warmongers Floating All Alone in the Night

In space, being surrounded by a fleet of enemy warships means never having to say you're sorry.

Instead, it means having to say don't hurt me, don't feed me into your nutrient vats, don't lay your eggs in my vital organs, don't stick your probe in my orifices, and especially, don't fondle me with that tentacle I haven't had my shots.

None of which may be particularly pleasant, but it's all vastly preferable to "Sorry" if "Sorry" is pretty much the only other thing you've been able to say for weeks now.

For instance — just pulling an example out of thin air, you understand — let's say you're the richest, bravest, smartest, and classiest woman in known space. And let's say that several decades ago, when you thought you'd sworn off men forever, you inexplicably fell for and married some sweet dufus who is so, you should only excuse the expression, divorced from any of those qualities that some exobiologists hesitate to classify him as sentient. And let's say that after many, many years of connubial bliss, you all of a sudden can't stomach the carnal act anymore because of a certain perverse chain of events that began with him being kidnapped by a giant robot, and ended with you — trust us — giving birth to him nine months later. And let's say he's grown to some semblance of adulthood again and you've taken him on a long cruise through the uncharted star systems on the far side of the K'cenhowten Empire in a desperate and you've begun to think doomed attempt to rekindle the romantic spark that once upon a time led to you declaring him your Junior Space Ranger of Love. And let's say said romantic spark has eluded you, and you've both spent most of your subsequent days and nights miserably and awkwardly and inarticulately overapologizing for everything including the mutual ridiculous overabundance of apologies. Thus leading to such undignified circumlocutions as, "I'm sorry, I know you said you were sick of my apologies, and I shouldn't have apologized just then, but I felt I had to apologize for all the apologies I made for the apologies of three apologies ago."

In such a case, says Dear Abby, being surrounded by a fleet of hostile alien warships does at least have the salutatory effect of potentially giving you and your husband something new to talk about.

Still, Dejah Shapiro, ex-wife of the notorious interstellar criminal Ernst Vossoff, current wife of his one-time partner Karl Nimmitz, could have thought of better ways of bringing the spice back into her love life.

The threatening face on the view screen looked harmless enough, as grimly-visaged alien commanders go . . . which is to say it was relatively humanoid, possessed only the most rudimentary fangs, was colored a pretty and not at all nauseating shade of green, and flaunted none of the trendy barbed vampiric cilia that so many of the younger races seemed to rely upon to make their first impression these days. The fact that the owner of that face, Commodore S'Clri of the space station Ottoman 6, had just demanded her surrender if she failed to surrender within two minutes meant little to her, for Dejah believed in faces, and this was not a face capable of blowing her to smithereens prematurely.

She glanced over at her husband — whose own face was a completely hairless monument to incomprehension in all its myriad forms — and said: "Think, Karl, think. Have you ever, at any point in your travels, run into this species before? Can you come up with any reason why they'd imagine you a dangerous subversive notorious for his crimes against the state?"

Karl Nimmitz regarded the alien with the wounded dignity of a second-grader singled out by bullies in the schoolyard. "I dunno. Maybe it's something they ate. I always hallucinate after pastrami."

"You're always turned on after pastrami."

He shrugged. "Well, I hallucinate after something. If it's not pastrami, it's some other popular deli meat."

Since one of the many drawbacks of marriage to Karl Nimmitz was following his logic, Dejah actually wasted precious microseconds seriously considering the possibility that the alien armada had been driven mad by cold cuts. She shook her head to summon her temporarily missing IQ points back from the farthest reaches of her frontal lobes, winced as her neurons slipped back into position, wondered not for the first time in the last few weeks just what she was thinking when she'd fallen so madly in love with this man, and said: "What about those early years before we met? When you were partnered with my ex-husband, Ernst Vossoff? The two of you were fairly dangerous criminals, way back when."

"No, we weren't," said Nimmitz.

"Well, yeah, you weren't. But you tried."

"Ernst tried," said Nimmitz. "I just kept shaking my head and saying, I don't like this."

Which so closely resembled the carnal interludes in her marriage to Ernst that she had to shake her head again, to jettison the unwanted flashback. She pleaded: "But were any of your schemes political, my darling? Did you ever do anything to undermine a rightful government? Did you ever make speeches, print leaflets, draw caricatures, spout statistics, shout slogans, form conspiracies, form splinter groups within those conspiracies, assassinate the leaders of other conspiracies, recruit revolutionary armies, and march on capitols? Did you ever, even once, find yourself exiled to a cold and isolated planetoid with no companions save your small but loyal cadre of dedicated followers, with whom you spent day after day crocheting your flag into throw rugs while endlessly, endlessly dreaming of the day, sooner than anybody dared suspect, when the South, or whatever it was you called yourselves, would rise again?"

Nimmitz boggled. "I've never even registered to vote."

Dejah nodded without surprise. Of course not. There wouldn't have been any point, Karl Nimmitz being the kind of guy whose main reason for never entering a polling booth would have been the nigh-certainty of not being able to find his way back out. She chewed on her lower lip for a second or two, gaining both confidence and competence from the trace amounts of the IQ stimulant she applied with every morning's lip gloss, and then thoughtfully instructed the ship's hytex to contact Commodore S'clri. "Question," she said. "What do you intend on doing with my husband once you've got him? Torture? Brain-Rinse? Execution?"

Commodore S'clri looked shocked. "You must think us barbarians."

"I guess I'm just a silly goose that way. Bristling arrays

of weaponry tend to give me that kind of impression."

"It shouldn't," Commodore S'clri said sternly. "We're not motivated by revenge, only by our deep-rooted concern about all the subversive influences that threaten the universe at large. Which is why we plan to detain you both on the space-station Ottoman 6, where you'll have every chance to defend your husband against these charges — if you can."

Dejah and Nimmitz looked at each other.

Dejah said: "I don't know, Karl. I get the feeling these people set new standards for paranoia."

Nimmitz said: "Oh, good. I love Italian food."

Ottoman 6 turned out to be one of those old-fashioned cylindrical space stations so hopelessly out of date that they need to spin to produce gravity. Dejah had been on one of those once, as a young girl; but that one was a theme park called "Frontierland," where employees dressed as pioneers entertained the tourists by demonstrating the old, back-to-basics skills like patching hull breaches with dead bodies and creating random mutations with radiation leaks. By comparison, the builders of Ottoman 6 didn't seem to realize how ridiculously quaint it looked. The station was ten kilometers long, and constructed along lines that seemed to indicate a pathetic attempt at grandeur, even though to her eyes it resembled nothing more than a giant steel cigarette with gun ports.

According to her sensors it was home to half a million humans and aliens, floating all alone in the night. Terrific. The thought of that many people living in something so tacky gave her a migraine she could feel in her teeth.

However, it did appear to be thriving; even as she and Nimmitz emerged from their space yacht into the dim light and recycled air of station customs, she spotted representatives of over fifty different species, at least half of which she actually recognized and one or two of which she genuinely respected. She saw a pair of sway-backed Riirgaans struggling to unload a gigantic crate while a vendor of used anti-gravity luggage-handling equipment tried to sell them a slightly bruised box-lightener; a Coriggian pickpocket being swatted away from the facial pouches of a fat marsupial from Durgiss IX; a lone human in black pants and gold velour pullover desperately serenading the crowd with what had to be the absolute worst rendition of a classical Beatles song in the history of music. It was pandemonium, but organized pandemonium, and it would have induced her to upgrade her estimation of this place two entire classifications were it not for the flickering overhead lights that instead made her wonder how come people smart enough to develop space travel were so rarely smart enough to change light bulbs.

As expected, an ostentatiously-armed security force was in place to greet them. Their leader resembled a julienne carrot with tentacles and male-pattern baldness; although his physiognomy was in no way humanoid, he must have had some traffic with humanity at one time or another, since he wore the tattered remains of a Space Patrol dress uniform, complete with empty arm-sleeves. And although his species did not possess legs, he did make a concession to the rules of human military bearing by producing a pair of shoes from his pocket and smartly clicking the heels together. "Welcome to Ottoman 6!" he barked. "I am the Security Chief, Mokyl Bariguldi. Which one of you is the male of your species?"

Nimmitz nudged Dejah. "Don't prompt me. I've been studying up on this one!"

Bariguldi blinked several times before turning his attention to Dejah. "Forgive me. This may be a rude question, but I sometimes have trouble keeping track of such things.

Was that truly as stupid as it seemed?"

Dejah's sigh was not exasperation, but genuine affection. "I'm afraid so."

"Astonishing. How did you ever achieve space flight?"

"Pure chance," Dejah lied. "Our distant ancestors tried to toss a salad during a labor day picnic, and accidentally developed a warp drive based on the unstable placement of croutons."

Bariguldi nodded as if that made literal sense. "I see. — So, to repeat: which one of you is the male?"

Nimmitz checked under his waistband. "Me."

"Then you're the human Karl Nimmitz?"

"What other versions have you found?" asked Nimmitz.

All intelligent species in the universe are subject to migraines, and for the past century or so, a disproportionate percentage of migraines have been suffered by those who tried to get a straightforward answer out of Karl Nimmitz. Bariguldi was no exception. When the vein in his forehead ceased throbbing, he said: "Mr. Nimmitz, you have been identified by an unimpeachable source as being one of the secret leaders of the Phantoms, an ancient and evil race intent on subverting all that is good and decent in the universe. Now, call us old-fashioned, no-fun stick-in-the-mud fuddy-duddies if you will, but we simply don't approve of that sort of thing around these parts. I have been ordered to place you in a holding cell under heavy guard, while escorting your mate here to the ruling council where she can hear the specifics of the charges levied against you. You can go peacefully or you go dead. It's up to you. Any questions?"

"Yeah," said Nimmitz. "What are those choices again?"

The ruling council of Ottoman 6 turned out to comprise four creatures of differing species. The first was Commodore S'clri himself, who sat at the head of the table, resplendent in a uniform of sequined overalls and slowly rotating bowtie; the second resembled a reptilian lemur with an attitude; the third, she initially mistook for a coffee stain that the custodial staff had somehow forgotten to mop up. Dejah was most interested in the fourth ambassador, who would have looked almost exactly like a human woman, but for bald pate and the thirteen-meter-tall pillar of gnarled bone that jutted upward from the top of her head. Whenever that ambassador nodded, everybody else in the room flinched, for fear of being impaled.

As Dejah took her seat, Commodore S'Clri took great care to introduce himself and the others. He was the ambassador from the Bursteenii Republic. The lemur with the attitude, who had a name best pronounced by strumming one's throat while burping, was the ambassador from the Eternal Holy Empire of the Gaaaaaaaaaaaa. The coffee stain was Ambassador Sanka of the Dikaffinates. The lady with the bone was the ambassador from Hocccch-ptui, and her name was Linda.

It was a good thing Dejah wasn't drinking water, because she would have committed a truly spectacular spit-take. "Linda? Did I actually hear you say your name was Linda?"

"Yes you did. Is there a problem?"

"Not much of one," Dejah admitted. "It's just that . . . well, it's not the kind of name I'd expect from an alien ambassador fifty light years from the nearest human colony."

"Are you saying that your species uses the name Linda too?"

"Yes. I am."

Linda considered that. "What a remarkable coincidence. Your language and ours must use a largely congruent assortment of phonemes. In such a case, it would not be totally unheard-of for parallel development to bring about the occasional, albeit totally irrelevant, evolution of identical words."

"But Linda, of all things —"

"Don't read too much into it. After all, it's only the shortened version of my full caste designation, which happens to be Linda Schwartz. And fascinating as such discussions of nomenclature may be, we really ought to be talking about your husband's pivotal role in the far-reaching conspiracy against all that is good and decent."

"I suppose you're right," said Dejah. "Because frankly, I'd like to know where you got the idea that my husband plays a pivotal role in anything. I mean, don't get me wrong. I'm madly in love with the man. Have been since the day I met him. He's a sweetheart. A genuine eleven. But I can't countenance villainy on a galactic scale on the part of a guy who not too long ago spent the better part of breakfast trapped with his lower lip stuck inside a toaster. The last time a telepath tried to read his mind, its own brain was blown out by the vacuum. If you really believe he's dangerous, you're either the most incompetent bunch of loonies I've ever met — and considering the man I was married to before this one, that's saying a lot — or this is nothing more than a shakedown for a bribe."

"We're not interested in your bribes," said Commodore S'Clri. "We don't even recognize your currency."

"Not even this?" Dejah flashed a wad of billion-credit notes.

"What's that?"

"Billion-credit notes!"

"Sorry. I didn't recognize them."

"I own stock in just about every financial institution

in the universe," Dejah persisted. "Adjusting the credits to the proper standard won't take more than five minutes by hytex. How much do you want? Five billion? Ten?"

"I appreciate the offer," Commodore S'clri said, "but I'm afraid we're dead serious about this one. We have every reason to believe that your husband isn't the blathering idiot he pretends to be, but instead a ruthless and wily agent of the ancient and evil race that's been responsible for everything bad that's ever happened to everybody since the dawn of time."

"I know you don't know humans very well, but the expression on my face is called aghast."

"Is that what you call it? A ghast? That little pointy thing between your eyes is a ghast?"

"Not exactly," said Dejah. "That's a nose. Aghast is —"

"Well, whatever. We honestly believe that you don't know the true extent of your husband's villainy, but no doubt you'll feel differently once we explain it to you as it was explained to us."

"I doubt it," said Dejah, "but I'm willing to listen."

"There's a race out there, older than the stars . . ."

"Unlikely so far. No stars, no planets. No organic molecules, no place to evolve. But please continue. I find this fascinating."

Commodore S'Clri frowned in irritation, and started over. "There's a race out there, older than the stars, blacker than the darkest night . . ."

"Not just unlikely but inherently nonsensical. Go ahead."

The members of the ruling council traded looks of aggrieved consternation until Linda leaned forward and said: "You know, it's going to be hard enough sharing all of this lengthy exposition without you sitting there making fun of every other sentence."

"Deal with it," Dejah said genially.

"Very well. The Phantoms are so far ahead of us that to them we resemble the lowly amoeba, and yet they hate us with every fibre of their beings . . ."

"Which sounds good," Dejah agreed, "until you realize how petty they'd have to be to hate amoebas."

Once again the ruling council displayed massive frustration. The lemur thing puffed out its cheeks to some four times their original radius and asked, "Are you like this all the time?"

"Only when I'm listening to stories that don't make sense."

"Be that as it may," Commodore S'Clri said sternly, "I would prefer that you withhold your withering critical analysis until after I've finished, or I'll never get through this."

"Very well," said Dejah. "Go ahead."

"Ahem. The Phantoms, as we call them, are the most mysterious and the most evil race that ever lived. Nobody has ever seen one; nobody has ever discovered where they're from. All we know is that they move silently and invisibly, leaving no physical evidence but the subtle havoc they leave in their wake." He paused in mid-story, and peered at Dejah. "You're biting your lip. Is there any significance to that?"

"Yes. It's something my people do to avoid laughing out loud."

"In any event, when the Phantoms last struck openly, sometime before the dawn of recorded history, the only thing that prevented them from bulldozing the entire universe and erecting a parking lot in its place was the stalwart opposition of their ancestral enemies, the Strazins, who got all the other indigenous races of the time to put aside all their centuries of hatred and distrust —"

"And sing Kumbaya," Dejah suggested.

"— and unite to drive the loathsome Phantoms back

to whatever hellish spawning pit they called home. It was a long-fought battle, that succeeded only because the Strazins were there to guide the forces of goodness, and when it achieved great and glorious victory, the result was a shining new era of peace and brotherhood that lasted at least six months before the surviving allies went to war to determine just who among them was going to pay the bills for all this. By which point the Strazins had departed, to some unspecified destination beyond the stars. And in the eons that followed, all records of the Phantoms and the war to defeat them faded into the sands of prehistory . . . forever lost, forever forgotten . . . with neither the Phantoms nor their ancient enemies the Strazins ever seen again . . . until now."

"Dum de dum dum!" hummed Dejah. "Dum de dum dum . . . *dum!*"

"Yes," Commodore S'clri managed, "it was the last surviving Strazin . . . a being so ancient and venerable and so wise that our people have wittily nicknamed him the Ancient Venerable Wise Being. He is Lord Vostoi, last of the Strazins, and he traveled here, to this space station, to this station of commerce and diplomacy, to this last best hope for peace, to teach us the old histories . . . remind us of those old forgotten days . . . and warn us that the Phantoms were back."

When Ambassador Linda nodded, her thirteen-meter tall pillar of bone seemed dangerously close to toppling. "He is the one who told us that your husband was their leader."

"So," Dejah said, "let's summarize, only without the purple prose. You've gathered together to fight a phantom race that none of you have ever seen, that until recently none of you have ever heard about, that left absolutely no physical evidence of its existence, that doesn't even have a forwarding address, or I'd wager a two-line listing in the

Official Galactic Registry of Genocidal Warmongers Looking For Work, that you only know about because you were told about them by some other guy you know nothing about who just happened to show up one day with some war stories. This is the evidence that's led you to declare my husband, a sweet guy and a phenomenal lover but as a threat about as formidable as pollen, the hidden mastermind behind this glorified rumor. Am I more or less correct about this?"

"Well, put like that," Linda conceded, "it does sound pretty flimsy. But we don't tell it as persuasively as the Ancient Wise One does. Talk to him, why don't you. Then come back here and we'll talk further."

"Fair enough," said Dejah. "What's his address?"

The Strazin lived in a specially shielded chamber in a section of Ottoman 6 primarily inhabited by the wealthy; that section wholly identical to the sections primarily inhabited by the poor, save for the porcelain lawn jockeys that stood guard outside the sliding doors to each airtight compartment.

It allowed her in only as far as the first airlock, then wafted in on a pillar of blinding light, casting little rainbow reflections in all directions, which would have looked impressive if it hadn't made the lighting look like some cheap backwater disco. Strange discordant music accompanied its approach, in a manner that reminded Dejah of a spastic and inebriated orchestra absent-mindedly tuning up the wrong end of their wind horns; there was no discernable tune or melody, but if you had no discernable sense of rhythm you could dance to it. The music did not seem to be coming from the Strazin itself — which appeared to be a seven-foot-tall, rotating egg — so much as from somewhere inside her own head. That meant it had to be either some kind of advanced psionic communication system, or a harmonic wave front that made her pick up ancient radio broadcasts on her tooth fillings. Either way it deserved to be respected . . . and for the very first time it occurred to Dejah that it just might know what it was talking about.

When it spoke, its voice possessed the distorted, underwater quality of a Universal Translating System straining to express thoughts too alien for Dejah's human mind to parse. Based on the phraseology it came up with, Dejah had to assume that the device was working at the absolute limits of its capabilities.

◊ Hello there, cutie ◊

She was unruffled. "Hello there, eggman. I'm the walrus."

◊ I am Lord Vostoi of the Strazin ◊ We are the Protectors ◊ We fought the Phantoms at the beginning of time ◊ We beat their ectoplasmic butts ◊ We can do it again ◊ Rah rah sis boom bah ◊

Dejah said: "Brave sentiments coming from a giant egg."

◊ This is not an egg ◊ This is my life-support capsule ◊ My encounter suit, if you will ◊ I wear it to protect me from the ravages of this atmosphere ◊ And to hide my true appearance ◊ For if any of you were to cast your eyes upon me ◊ It would drive you mad ◊ Mad ◊ Mad I tell you ◊ Mad ◊

"Well, from what I can see, you've already been showing your face to too many people around here, because a bigger group of loonie-tunes I never saw."

◊ Insane times require insane people ◊ just as stupid times require stupid people ◊ and annoying times require annoying people ◊ and flatulent times ◊ . . . well perhaps it's best that we not get into that ◊ either way it is the principal lesson of history ◊ next to the folly of thinking you won't have Nixon to kick around any more ◊ In any event, this space station ◊ and these people ◊ are the last hope of the cosmos ◊

The war for survival will be fought here ◊

"The war against what? These phantom whatchamacallits?"

◊ Yes ◊ The Phantom Whatchamacallits ◊ Though we usually just call them the Phantoms ◊ The Phantom Whatchamacallits being too unwieldy a phrase ◊ It doesn't roll lightly off the tongue ◊ even of those species that evolve tongues in the first place ◊ In any event ◊ They are preparing a new offensive ◊ a new war against all other life in the universe ◊ and they must be stopped ◊ starting with your husband ◊

"Funny you should bring them up, buddy. It's precisely what I want to talk to you about."

◊ Your husband Karl Nimmitz is not what he seems ◊ He cannot be ◊ No one man can be that stupid ◊ He is the secret leader of the Phantoms ◊

"That's ridiculous," Dejah said. "What proof do you have?"

◊ I am a billion years old and I live in an egg ◊ Would I do this at my age if it wasn't true? ◊ Think, Dejah ◊ Think ◊ You are the smartest, wealthiest and most powerful woman in the known galaxy ◊ You embody excellence in all its forms ◊ You are the apex of human achievement ◊ You are the ideal toward which all members of your species strive ◊ Now think about your husband and the impression he gives visiting dignitaries when he accidentally swallows the silverware ◊ Why would a woman like you love a man like him? ◊ Is it sensible for you to be married to a man whose favorite indoor sport is pushing all the buttons in elevators? ◊ Or are you being controlled by the Phantoms? ◊ Is this all just a plot to lull you into complacency as he affects your industries, undermines your defenses, and makes you less than you can be? ◊

For most of her marriage, Dejah would have been able to come up with some brilliant response to that. Today it took her several seconds just to recover. "It's . . . love! There's never any explanation for love! You should see who my aunt Cathy married! She was a galactically renowned concert violinist, he was an unshaven slob who wore dirty t-shirts and picked his feet in finer restaurants! It didn't mean he was some kind of evil alien invader!"

The Strazin hovered gravely. *◊ As a matter of fact, it does ◊ We know of your step-uncle ◊ His name was Oscar Kruger ◊ and among those who truly see the structure of the universe ◊ he was known as the Reaver of Worlds ◊*

"Oh, I refuse to listen to this! Uncle *Oscar?* An old guy with cigar breath and a pot belly? A guy whose biggest crime in life was wearing mismatched bunny slippers? Who are you trying to fool?"

◊ In your heart of hearts, you know this is true ◊ He was the Reaver of Worlds ◊ and your husband Karl Nimmitz is the Ravager of Stars ◊ He must be placed on trial for his crimes against intelligent life ◊ He must be forced to tell what he knows ◊ And you must cease your futile efforts to defend him ◊

"I can't do that! He's my husband!"

The Strazin turned its eggy back and floated back into the mists from whence it came. *◊ Whatever ◊*

It was a significantly shaken Dejah Shapiro who made her way to the internment compound of Ottoman 6. The sudden nagging doubts had left her a pale shadow of her former self; indeed, the strain evident on her face had in the past half hour alone had caused her to slip from Most Beautiful Woman In the Galaxy all the way down to Number Seven. The deterioration was not yet visible to the naked eye, and indeed would have been almost impossible to discern with state-of-the-art instruments, but Dejah was aware of it — and she didn't like the rate at which she could feel herself plummeting toward that humiliating eighth slot.

Even so, she didn't look even remotely as disturbed as security chief Mokyl Bariguldi, who sat holding his head in the spongelike appendages he possessed instead of hands.

"What's wrong?" asked Dejah.

There were several false starts before Bariguldi managed to find his voice. "I was just interrogating your husband."

"And?"

"I can't stand his non-sequiturs!" Bariguldi wailed. "My head's exploding!"

Forget Number Eight. Dejah felt herself wither all the way down to Number Twelve. "Can I speak with him, please?"

Unable to face the thought of facing the captive Nimmitz again, Bariguldi whimpered, attempted to rise, failed, and then, defeated, pressed a button on his control panel. A doorway appeared on the far wall. Dejah thanked him, and walked through, wishing this one of those hi-tech jails where it was possible to literally check one's migraine at the door.

As it turned out, the jail was so very low-tech that it actually had solid cell doors, with barred windows at visitor-height. This was a minor strike against the credibility of Ottoman 6. Most jail cells in the galaxy had open doorways equipped with teleportation grids that transported would-be escapees the exceedingly short distance back to the rear of their cells. This was a horrendously expensive system, of course, but it did possess the virtue of being horrendously frustrating — so much so that some prisoners develop a pathological hatred of doorways and actually refuse to leave their cells when their sentences are done. Jail cells with solid doors just didn't possess the same rehabilitative properties. Still, if her husband had to be in jail, she was glad to find him in the old-fashioned kind; knowing him, he would have exhausted himself walking through that door all day long, day after day, thinking only that he was trapped in some very long, very pointless, and very redundantly-decorated corridor.

If, she reminded herself, he was indeed the Karl Nimmitz she thought she knew . . .

As she approached his cell, he popped up in the window, gripping the steel bars in his hammy fists. "Dejah!"

She touched his hand protectively. "Karl. How are you holding up in there?"

"I don't like it, Dejah. It reminds me too much of jail."

"It is jail," she reminded him.

"Oh. Then it reminds me too much of school."

She massaged her temples with her fingers, suddenly understanding precisely how poor Bariguldi felt. "Karl . . . I've been talking to the people who run this place . . . and they've been telling me some very disturbing things."

"Like what?"

"Well, for instance . . . just picking one example at random . . . totally off the top of my head, you understand . . . they say you're the secret leader of the Phantoms, an ancient and evil race bent on universal conquest. What do you think of that, Karl?"

Nimmitz boggled. "What do you mean, what do I think of that?"

"I mean, what do you think of that?"

"What do *you* think of that?" he demanded.

"I asked you first."

"I know. I'm still wondering why you asked."

"Because," she said patiently, "I wanted to know what *you* thought."

"I can't tell you."

"And why not?"

"Because I've forgotten what we were talking about."

The throb between her temples grew louder. She passed Fifty on the beauty scale, while still accelerating downward. "Well, Karl . . . it's not like we've had the most normal marriage."

"What do you mean?"

Dejah bit her lip, wondering how best to put this. "Don't take this the wrong way, my darling . . . but most wives who genuinely love their husbands have some vague idea why. They can cite their mate's handsome features, or his tremendous courage, or his depth of character, or his brilliant wit, or his sense of style, or, failing all that, the occasional harder-to-define something that they can find nowhere else. You, on the other hand — while you may be a sweet guy — have the manners of a hamburger roll, the sophistication of a pickle slice, and the conversational skill of a large order of fries. We may have a happy meal, but I just can't see the nutritional value."

"Isn't it printed on the side of the carton?"

"I used to think it was the maternal quality in me," said Dejah. "After all, when I met you, you were partnered with my ex-husband, and in dire need of rescuing. The part of me that remembered being married to him identified with that. So I fell in love with you, practically at first sight. But I shouldn't still feel that way, after decades of watching you get your nose caught in elevator doors, should I? Especially not after having to give birth to your mitochondrially induced clone!"

He gripped the bars more tightly. "What are you saying?"

"That if you *are* the secret leader of an ancient race bent on universal conquest, then you probably have resources greater than those you allow anybody else to see. You probably want to be married to me because of my wealth and influence, and you probably know subtle mind-control techniques designed to keep me devoted to you, despite what should now be incredible dissatisfaction with the state of our relationship. Is that possible, Karl? Is it?"

Nimmitz said: "I don't know. I guess. If it is I sure don't know about it. I just thought you liked calling me your Junior Space Ranger. I sure liked hearing you say it. — Who the hell made up that stuff, anyway?"

"Some guy dressed like an egg."

"I don't usually listen to guys dressed like eggs. There's no telling where they've been. Have you known this guy long?"

"No. Just met him. His name's Lord Vostoi, last of the Strazins."

"Lord what?"

"Vostoi. V-O-S . . ." She closed her mouth, and remained silent for a full five seconds. "Why, that miserable bastard."

There are, in the universe, only three forces that cannot be resisted, that cannot be fought, and cannot be denied.

One of those is entropy.

Another is the mysterious binding force known only as Fhahr, which makes The Other Line move faster than The One You're On.

The third is Dejah Shapiro when she's truly and irrevocably pissed off.

The inhabitants of Ottoman 6 got their first taste of that when she barreled out of the security corridor, with all the speed and determination of a Batrilsian Rhino in full charge. Even the aliens that had had never seen a human face before, and therefore had no otherwise explicable way of interpreting her expression as that of A Woman Whose Way You Most Definitely Do Not Want to Block, scurried for cover; and when a security guard attempted to block her entrance to the diplomatic wing she merely snarled and flicked him over the railing and onto the crowd below with the most disdainful twitch of her perfectly sculpted fingernail.

She caught up with Lord Vostoi at the convenience store where two of the corridors branched, wholly gratified to catch him in the act of buying toothpaste, beef jerky, and the latest issue of *Villainy Today.*

It was hard to tell through the egg, but he may have blanched when he saw the expression on her face. *◊ Uh Oh ◊*

She grabbed the egg with both hands and, putting her weight into it, spun it as fast as she could. That was pretty darn fast: The murkily translated speech being broadcast from inside took on a distinctively nauseated quality: *◊ Stop ◊ Don't Do This ◊ We Can Still Make A Deal ◊ You Don't Know What Kind of Business Opportunity This Is ◊ These Pathetic Chumps Will Believe Anything ◊*

She reached out and clapped a Shapiro Industries pocket vibrational resonance bomb to the spinning egg. The armless Vostoi, who could not remove it any other way, zipped over to the far end of the store and attempted to scrape it off against the Automatic Teller, but by then the hairline cracks on his outer shell had already begun to spread, in an explosive lightning-pattern that stopped only when the egg exploded, littering the overpriced canned goods with shrapnel.

The figure that fell from the egg was not a wise and ancient elder of the universe. It wasn't even a newborn baby chick.

It was Ernst Vossoff — notorious interstellar criminal, ex-partner of Karl Nimmitz, and ex-husband of Dejah Shapiro.

Dejah went off. "You cad! You dirtbag! You scuzzbucket! You no-neck geek! You monument to entropy!

You sack of neutronic phlogiston! You slimy anti-phylogenic reverse-evolution crud! You malfunctioning anti-gravity commode! You fault-line in the tectonic plate of life! You previously undiscovered and completely useless subatomic particle! You free-flying cloud of intestinal vapor! You not very interesting conversationalist! You cosmic redundancy! You living disproof of the kindness of God! You excrement of the Lovecaftian elder Gods! You —"

"Excuse me," said the proprietor of the convenience store. "This is a family establishment. I'm afraid we can't have —"

"*Expel it out your third eye, blueskin! Call station security if you don't like it! In fact, activate your cameras and send the hytex feed to Bariguldi! I want him to see this anyway!*"

Vossoff tried to pull a concealed weapon from his belt. Dejah recognized it as a Bettelhine Munitions sonic grenade and batted it away with a single flick of her hand. It went off near the porno magazines, filling the room with confetti-sized pictures of alien invertebrates doing obscene things in vacuum chambers. Vossoff reached for another weapon. Dejah reached down, seized one end of his giant walrus moustache in each hand, and yanked his helpless flailing form off the floor. All the WAY off the floor, so his feet kicked and flailed above the deckplate: Dejah being not only a tall girl, but a remarkably fit one.

"You almost had me," she snarled. "Incorporating my Uncle Oscar in your cock-and-bull story — that was brilliant. I couldn't imagine any other way an enigmatic billion-year-old alien would even know who my Uncle Oscar was, so it made the whole scenario almost believable. I never even considered the possibility that I was speaking to somebody who'd actually *met* my Uncle Oscar!"

Dangled from the hair on his upper lip, Vossoff was helpless to do anything but cringe. "Dejah . . . my one true love . . . I don't mean to criticize . . . but this isn't exactly the most . . . pleasant . . . sensation . . . I've ever had. Would you please. . . ?"

"Ernst, if you don't confess everything right now, and I mean the instant I lower you to the deck, I will introduce your sorry behind to three hundred and fifty-six sensations that make this little exercise in excruciating agony look like a backrub."

His eyes widened. "Three . . . hundred . . . and fifty-six?"

"Starting with creative uses for that can-opener over there."

"Interesting," he managed, in the last gasp of his defiance. "I wouldn't . . . have been able . . . to come up with . . . more than . . . two hundred and twenty."

She introduced him to number fifty-three. He wheezed and said: "Fascinating . . . I wouldn't . . . have thought of . . . *that* one . . . in a million years . . ."

"Will you confess?"

". . . absolutely . . ."

Hating the civilized instincts that required her to show mercy, Dejah reluctantly lowered him to the deck. "Now, talk. What are you doing here? Last we heard of you, twenty years ago, you and two other equally reprehensible pieces of space-vermin had been reduced to submicroscopic size and imprisoned inside some spaceman's liver!"

Vossoff massaged his sore lip. "Indeed. And a more pointlessly dreary place I've never known — even Fyliss IV and New Pylthothus, nightmarish as they were, had their share of gothic panache. Fortunately, about six standard years ago, when that particular diminutive, and I should add, thanks to your Neolithic husband, totally fingerless body of mine was finally murdered at the hands of my fellow submicroscopic castaways, the mitochondria responsible for our plight took pity on my helplessness and reincarnated me as the parasitic twin attached to the back of an Arcturian hippo. I spent another two months staring up the sky as my host grazed amid the tall grass of the savannah, and I'd be there still had the beast not been shot by some big-game hunter either too moral or too aesthetically picky to mount me on the wall with the rest of his hard-won trophy. After the surgery, I made my way to New Vegas, where I — hey! *Hey!* Stop that! That hurts!"

Dejah put him down again. "Now tell me what you're doing here."

"Isn't it obvious?" Vossoff sneered. "Some people will listen to any line of paranoid conspiracy bullshit as long as it comes from a mysterious enigmatic figure in an all-concealing encounter suit. Admittedly, not *many* people — you have no idea how many space colonies sent me packing before I finally ran into one inhabited by a sufficiently gullible pack of rubes. But once that happened, my future fortunes were assured."

"But the Phantoms, Ernst? The Phantoms!?!?"

"Why not? It's a perfectly good story. I didn't even make it up; I just appropriated it from some broken-down, liver-spotted, wild-haired old rummy who I heard using it to cadge free drinks in a spaceport bar. He claimed it was true, too, but didn't have enough imagination to exploit it properly, like I did. And corny or not, you can't argue with my results. I've been skimming ten percent off the top of this place's operating expenses for the better part of two standard years now, and until you came along, was well on my way to becoming the wealthiest sentient in this sector."

"Which would have been enough for you," Dejah said, "if we hadn't passed through the celestial neighborhood, activating your burning thirst for revenge against me and Karl."

"Oh, sure. That goes without saying. Making you doubt him — and precipitating what is probably the inevitable decline of your marriage to that inane cretin — was worth it all by itself. But that wasn't all I was after. I planned to milk that beetle-brained bozo's trial for all it was worth — bilking you for court costs and legal fees, selling rights to the hytex feed to the media conglomerates of ten thousand different planets, engaging lawyers and legal experts to endlessly discuss the case on talk shows, starting an entire branch of the interstellar publishing industry just to churn out book after book on the proceedings, introducing months on meaningless side-controversies just to keep it going. The way I figured it, I would have surpassed you in wealth in about a year."

"Assuming you managed to drag out such a farcical trial for a year."

"Why not?" Vossoff said. "Your celebrated ancestor did."

That did it. Dejah Shapiro was about to introduce her hated ex-husband to each and every agonizing sensation she could think of, when all of a sudden a soft hand grabbed her wrist from behind. She whirled, expecting an attack — and saw instead the calm but sheepish face of Ambassador Linda Schwartz, who she almost didn't recognize because her bald pate and her twelve-meter-tall pillar of gnarled bone had somehow been replaced by a much more attractive, and probably much more manageable, darling pageboy-do.

"Men," Linda sympathized.

"Uh . . . yeah. Say, didn't you used to have a thirteen-meter tall pillar of bone protruding from the top of your head?"

Linda nodded gravely. "Yes."

"I knew it looked ridiculous, but I just assumed it was normal for your species."

Linda cried out in scandalized amazement. "*That* thing? Heavens, no! That would be horrible!"

"What happened to it, then?"

"It went away," said Linda.

It was sometime later. The tidal wave of apologies and victory parties now finally over and done with, and Commodore S'Clri's offer of free Ottoman 6 snow-globes, teddy bears, and souvenir t-shirts politely declined, Dejah Shapiro and her husband Karl Nimmitz hurried back into their space-yacht to take their leave. They did not dawdle leaving Ottoman 6 space-dock; indeed, once they were out in open space, Dejah paused just long enough to take a last fond look at their old friend Ernst Vossoff, who was working off his massive debt by polishing the giant space station's outer hull. As Ottoman 6 was a big place, and he'd only been given a supply of toothbrushes to work with, he'd probably be performing this community service for a long, long time. But that was okay: as he'd been sealed inside a tamper-proof vacuum suit with an infinitely recycling supply of food, water, and air, he wouldn't want to prolong that time with unnecessary rest and recreation. Commodore S'Clri estimated that even at ten hours a day, it would probably take him forty standard years to polish the entire hull from end to end — by which point, with any luck, even he might think twice about ever again giving advice while dressed like an egg.

Dejah, who sat behind the controls, watched Vossoff work for all of thirty seconds before the space-suited figure abruptly stood up and waved his fist at her. Sound didn't have to travel in space for her to imagine she heard that familiar gravelly voice screaming at her in Slavic. She considered calling Karl to take a look, but decided against it — Nimmitz still didn't know his old partner was behind all this, and if he found out he'd probably insist on attempting a rescue.

That was one good thing about her husband, anyway: he certainly was loyal.

Loyal . . .

She was misting up, imagining herself unobserved, when her husband's voice startled her from behind. "Why are you crying, Dejah?"

She hurriedly blanked the view screen, so he wouldn't spot Vossoff. "Because I'm sad."

"Why sad?" he asked, as he sat in the empty seat beside her. "You took care of everything, just like you always do."

"Because I lost faith in you. Because we once had something so perfect and because it's been so long since it was perfect and because for a few short hours they actually made me think you were secretly the devious megalomaniacal leader of an ancient alien species plotting universal domination. I can't imagine you ever forgiving me."

"You can't?" said Nimmitz. "Really?"

"Of course not! You must be furious at me!"

"No, I'm not," he said. "I'm flattered."

Stunned, she looked at his utterly guileless eyes, and for just ten seconds wondered if the story of the Phantoms could be true after all. It could be, after all; as Ernst himself admitted, he hadn't made it up himself, but only plagiarized it from some old guy he'd encountered in a bar. And when all was said and done, it was just as reasonable to believe her husband a mind-controlling mastermind, forcing her to love him against her will, as it was to think that a woman like her could spend the days and nights of her life head-over heels gaga with Karl the hulking vessel for a single-digit IQ. Thanks to Vossoff — who'd finally succeeded in something for the first time in his long and misbegotten life — part of her would never be sure which scenario was the right one. All she knew was that there was only one way to banish the doubts.

She smiled, once again The Most Beautiful Woman In the Galaxy. "I know it's been a while, honey, but as soon as I set course corrections, we're playing barbarian and geisha."

"Really?"

"Yes. Really."

Nimmitz hooted. "Oh boy! My favorite! Props!"

Which was almost, but not quite, the end of it.

Because that night, after she fell asleep thinking, It's all Right, It's Over, He's No Devious Alien Mastermind, He's Just Karl, after all . . .

. . . Nimmitz waited until he was absolutely certain she was unconscious. Then he rose, padded to the control room, warmed up the communications console, and sent the secret coded message to his fellow conspirators at their next scheduled port of call . . .

TO BE CONTINUED!

Just a Couple of Ruthless Interstellar Assassins Discussing Real Estate Investments at a Twister Game the Size of a Planet

When throwing cocktail parties large enough to occupy entire continents, it is always important to remember that access to the buffet table is an issue important enough for the fighting of wars.

Take the billions of well-wishers who crowded the catering-hall planet Desiarnaz to attend the surprise birthday bash for Dejah Shapiro, the richest, smartest, and most beautiful woman in the known universe. The planet's recommended seating capacity, along the glittering crystal plain that its management rented as a dance floor, was no more than ten thousand; the stargate invitations her husband had sent to everybody with even the slightest connection to her life, not only in this era but throughout recorded history, numbered in the tens of billions. As a result, the teeming celebrants occupied every spare acre of land from the sweltering sand dunes of the desert Ethelmertz, to the fetid subtropical swamps of the peninsula Liddelrikki. They shivered with hypothermia on the glaciers, clung to the sides of mighty cliffs, waded through waist-deep water in the flood plains, and determinedly made small talk on the thundering slopes of its actively erupting volcanoes. With more guests arriving at every moment, a few even resorted to treading water in its storm-tossed seas. It was, all in all, a grand experiment in packing as many sentient beings into as small as land area as could possibly be accomplished . . . a folly rendered unimaginably worse by the party-planning skills of her husband Karl Nimmitz, who had honestly believed he could feed all these people with a single plate of cold cuts arrayed on a folding table somewhere near the forty-seventh parallel.

Not everybody found this unreasonable. After all, there were some among them who had been at the original Woodstock and found this infinitely more organized. And you couldn't beat the planet for acoustics; no matter where the party guests stood, anywhere from sea to lurching sea, they could all hear the band just fine.

The guest of honor was not quite as happy . . .

Indeed, Dejah Shapiro's immediate reaction, as her yacht dropped out of hyperspace, was an appalled: "You did *what?*"

Karl Nimmitz, who had just joined her at the control deck after three or four hours of standing in the outer passageway trying to remember the proper procedure for using a doorknob, merely batted his cowlike eyes in adoration. "I invited all your friends to a surprise party for you. They're down on the planet."

Dejah sighed. It was a beautiful sigh. She was always

beautiful when she was exasperated. She was also beautiful when she was happy, when she was perturbed, when she was nauseated, when she was giddy, when she was exhausted, and when she was trying to remember a word at the tip of her tongue; there were no conceivable emotions, anywhere in her reactive lexicon, that did not enhance the nigh-infinite grandeur of her gorgeousity. But there was one highly specific expression that by some perverse genetic whim showed her off to an advantage that left all the others far behind — and it may not have been pleasant, and it may not have been fair, but she'd always looked most beautiful when she was Totally Flabbergasted. Naturally, her eventful marriage to Karl Nimmitz (sweet guy, possessor of the galaxy's single lowest IQ, and retired lackey of the notorious interstellar criminal Ernst Vossoff) had left her more radiant than ever before. Reaching a new height of pulchritude even as she tried to massage away the migraine pounding between her temples, she faced her husband with considerable dread and asked: "When on Earth, or any other convenient world, did you have time to plan a surprise party?"

"After we left Ottoman Six," Nimmitz specified. "Right after you fell asleep. I secretly accessed the ship's hytex, reserved the planet, ordered cold cuts, and sent stargate invitations to everybody in your personal database."

"Stargate invitations?"

"You know. Anybody who receives one and believes that they might want to go gets transported there automatically across the hyperspace translink."

"I know what they are, Karl, as well as how expensive they are, but . . . well, you're very sweet, and I really do appreciate it . . . but as you know, I'm the single wealthiest sentient in the known universe. My personal database is huge. It includes not only my three or four billion dearest friends — which would be crowded enough — but also three or four billion who would happily throttle me if they ever had the opportunity, as well as three or four billion notable for not having an opinion one way or the other. It also includes literally tens of thousands of famous historical personalities, from all eras and walks of life, thanks to my personal experiments in time travel. Please tell me you adjusted for selectivity before sending the invitations? Pretty please? Karl?"

Nimmitz blinked several times and said: "What did you mean last week, when you said that thing about the happy meal?"

The pause that followed was not quite long enough for the evolution of universes.

It ended with Dejah scanning the planetary surface with her ship's instruments, her crest falling with every instant. When she was done, she sighed heavily. "Let's summarize. Billions of people transported without warning to a world too small to accommodate them, without sufficient food or water. As a result, irreversible ecological damage, a body count in the upper seven figures, the headaches involved with having to figure out a way to evacuating all the survivors not only safely but without insult, liabilities greater than the treasuries of most sentient species, and legal repercussions with the potential to keep my most expensive lawyers working double overtime for decades."

"You're mad," Nimmitz perceived.

Dejah rubbed her forehead. "I'm not mad —"

"Yes, you are. I can always tell."

"It's not about whether I'm mad. It's about . . ." She gazed into his cowlike, injured-puppy eyes, and melted. "Ah well. At least it won't be the worst party I've ever been to."

Nimmitz's chin trembled. "It won't?"

She patted him on the hand. "Of course not, honey.

It would have to be about ten times worse than this to match my wedding to Ernst . . ."

But the universe was gearing up to correct that deficiency.

The vessel emerging from hyperspace on the opposite side of the planet, a creation of the universally loathsome Bettelhine Munitions Corporation, was notable for the single-mindedness with which it reeked evil from every rivet. It didn't just "cruise through space" — it "savagely ripped through the aether with the pitiless predatory grace of the marauding blood-beast." It didn't just "move into a geosynchronous orbit 44,000 kilometers above the planet" — it "found a place where it could lurk like a vulture waiting for its prey to cough up internal organs." It didn't just "make an infinitesimal course correction to adjust for local gravitational anomalies" — it "viciously hunted down the imperfections in its navigational systems and eradicated them with sadistic glee." The *Jehosophat*, as it was known, was a specter of absolute darkness, an aesthetic abomination, and a mockery of everything that was good and decent.

Which was all a fairly accurate description of its pilot as well.

His name was Ernst Vossoff, as he was notable not only for having one of the bushiest walrus moustaches in known space, but also for being a notorious space rogue wanted for capital crimes on a hundred planets, for being a lousy tipper despised by waitresses on a thousand more, for being the only thief in the history of crime who was both ruthless and shortsighted enough to travel five minutes into the future into the future and swindle himself out of his life savings, and — most relevantly, for the purposes of this account — for being both the estranged ex-partner of the unimaginably doltish Karl Nimmitz and the estranged ex-husband of the unimaginably wealthy Dejah Shapiro. Thanks to the aftermath of his last several encounters with ex-wife and ex-partner, who were now intolerably married to each other, he was also notable for an unpleasant facial tic that resembled the result of a civil war pitting eyebrow against upper lip. Said tic being especially violent as he aimed the complete offensive capability of his warship at the overcrowded revelry on the planet below.

He wished he could kill everybody down there more than once. Twice would not be enough. Three would not be excessive. Four would be disappointing. Five would be a mere canapé. Six would not even begin to satisfy him. He wanted to parboil that planetary crust again and again and again, bringing everybody back to life again and again and again, so he could continue to bomb them to putty again and again and again. Alas, the way this universe worked, he would only get to bomb them once, thus totally exhausting his personal list of things to do today. Just thinking about the inevitable anticlimax was enough to make his eyeballs hurt . . . but not too much.

Dreading the inevitable anticlimax, he reached toward the firing button . . .

. . . only to hesitate when a young blonde woman only four inches tall materialized there, waggled her finger, and said: "No. You don't want to do that."

The surprise party Karl Nimmitz had thrown for his lovely wife was deficient in one respect not already covered in her lengthy recitation of all the myriad ways he had screwed up this time. In the absence of sufficient food, sufficient water, sufficient standing room, and sufficient access to the mistress of honor, this particular inadequacy went largely unmentioned except for a couple of guys from some planet's equivalent of the East Village who happened to be predisposed toward keeping track of such things: namely, that for a trendy cocktail party, it didn't seem to have anywhere near the usual number of potted ferns.

The main reason for this, of course, is that potted ferns appear almost exclusively in corners, and since the entire party took place outside, there were no corners to be had except on the bodies of those party guests whose species had evolved with right angles. And there weren't many of those, since this wasn't a party for squares.

Factoring them aside, there was only one potted fern on the entire planet.

It was an admirable specimen, as such things go: tall and leafy, and altogether fernlike, as such things go. It took the jostling of drunken party guests with an equanimity that even most members of its species would have done well to emulate; not expressing anger or angst or murderous rage of any kind, even when one boorish guest extinguished his cigar on one of its leaves. It didn't seem to mind that nobody talked to it, and nobody noticed it; it certainly didn't complain about the communal lack of appreciation for its determination to heroically decorate this entire party all by itself, without any other ferns to lend moral support or balance out the room.

Some people might have said that this was because it was as mindless as any other plant.

Certain paranoid others might have theorized that it was simply lying low, waiting for the proper moment to strike.

It was a matter open for debate. But anybody who genuinely wished to determine the truth would have to factor in two very basic, but very important observations: one, that it was, after all, just a fern. And two, that it was holding a bomb.

Ernst Vossoff took the arrival of the tiny little woman extraordinarily well, considering; considering; his twitch accelerated only enough to make his face look like a planet being scoured by a worldwide thunderstorm. He did not fire the weapons he had trained on the planet. Instead, he just stared at the diminutive stranger aboard his ship, and wondered how best to describe her. Thin? Well, yes . . . at that size she'd just about have to be. Long-legged? Well, maybe by proportion with the rest of her; in objective terms they were each as long as his index fingers. Long-haired? Same observation; it fell to halfway down her back, but in absolute terms wasn't even long enough to scandalize a marine drill sergeant. Beautiful? Well, maybe. He supposed. His eyes were bothering him and he wasn't up to squinting. She was dressed in a form-fitting yellow jumpsuit, with what appeared to be miniscule black polka dots, and she wore a (proportionately) big floppy hat with a hummingbird feather that rose high above her head in an explosion of color that did not escape garishness by being infinitesimal.

Vossoff cleared his throat. "You, dear, are an interesting development."

"Thank you," she said. "I must admit, you look fairly fascinating yourself. Love the moustache."

He preened. "And well you should."

"What exactly do you use to give that iridescent sheen? Moustache wax or rocket fuel?"

"Rocket fuel," he said. "I find that the fumes stimulate my genius. And what exactly brings such a perceptive and discerning woman to my weapons console?"

"I was wondering: before you press that doomsday button, can we talk?"

"I daresay we passed that point in our mutual evolution some time ago. May I assume you're a hologram of some kind?"

"That's right," said the young lady. "I'm being projected by the cruiser fifty kilometers off your starboard bow. The real me just popped out of hyperspace and spotted you in your gothic black number, about to commence saturation bombing. I thought I'd try to talk you out of it."

"Why? Do you have some objection?"

"Not in a moral sense, no. I've done it myself a few times. However, if you do incinerate this planet and everybody on it, you will be interfering with certain contractual obligations very near and dear to my personal financial structure, so I will therefore be obliged to incinerate you in retribution."

Vossoff actually felt a tingle. "That would tend to throw a damper on my attendant feelings of personal triumph."

"My point exactly."

"Perhaps if I explain my justification, my dear. — You see, the guest of honor of that particular planet-wide blowout down there is my ex-wife, Dejah Shapiro, a very cruel and demented woman who has in the recent historical past arranged for my imprisonment at hard labor. Thanks to her machinations, I was to spend the next six lifetimes locked in a recycling suit outside the space station Ottoman Six, scrubbing the outer hull with a toothbrush; I would be there still if her inane boob of a paramour hadn't seen fit to send me a free get-out-of-jail card in the form of an stargate invitation to this little soiree."

The little lady nodded. "I figured it had to be something like that."

"You did?"

"Of course. It's the oldest story in the book."

"It is?"

"Well, in some books, anyway. How come you're arriving here by starship, instead of popping in among the various well-wishers below?"

"Because nobody who's spent any substantial period of time with Karl Nimmitz would ever be stupid enough to willingly teleport himself to coordinates programmed in by him. When I received my invitation, which was printed on abominably tacky stationery, by the way, I took the liberty of reprogramming it before I sent my RSVP. As a result, I was transported not to that upper-crust hog wallow down below, but to the main showroom of the Bettelhine Munitions Corporation . . . where I wasted no time liberating this little death machine for my own nefarious purposes. In any event, the point remains the same. After all I've suffered at the hands of that nouveau-riche harpy, incinerating the planet and everybody on it is not just an insane act of revenge; it is a moral imperative that deserves applause and not scorn."

"I certainly agree," the beautiful little hologram said. "I suppose that if I were in your place I'd probably want to push that button myself. — However, if you refrain from incinerating that planet and everybody on it, I get to search for a certain party guest who's worth fifty billion credits if taken alive."

Vossoff fingered the tips of his moustache. "Fifty billion credits."

"Give or take a planetary treasury or two."

"Excuse me," Vossoff said. He turned his back on her and made a scale of his hands. On one hand he weighed more wealth than he could ever hope to acquire, in his lifetimes of illegal gain; on the other hand he weighed the sweet revenge he craved with an intensity that dwarfed gravity as one of the basic binding forces of the universe. On one hand there was no price sufficient enough to pay for all of his humiliation; mere self-respect demanded revenge, *now*. On the other hand . . . with billions of credits suddenly added to the equation . . . he just as suddenly found this woman thoroughly attractive.

"My dear . . . would you do me the extreme honor of joining me for lunch?"

At that very moment, on the teeming surface of the planet Desiarnaz, Dejah Shapiro found herself confronting a task that had stymied untold legions of party hostesses before her: finding a kind and ladylike way to get everybody to leave.

Simple adherence to form dictated that nobody among the billions of attendees would leave until after they had their legally mandated two minutes of charming small talk with the Guest of Honor. Alas, simple adherence to form did not consider the sheer number of guests at this particular party, and since most of the party participants would be not only long-dead from old age but also scattered trace elements blown to the four winds by the time Dejah would have been able to sufficiently scintillate even that small percentage of the teeming multitude thoughtful enough to bring along a marble loaf from Posselman's, let alone the far more numerous throngs who'd simply showed up with a bib and a spork and a determined tropism for the mythical buffet table, Dejah felt no compunction whatsoever about resorting to high technology.

Specifically, the Martha Stewart Paradigm. Once activated, this arcane meld of psionics, artificial intelligence, and tasteful catering projected a perfectly convincing 3-D simulation of Dejah at her most charming into the mind of each of every party guest fighting for a moment's air beneath an atmosphere rapidly turning maliforous from the billowing fumes of all their overapplied cologne. Said simulation was not only simply de-lighted to see each and every one of them, not only amused by each and every one of their tidbits of pointless and redundant gossip, not only acceptably flirtatious with everybody of any gender capable of responding in kind, not only willing to ask leading questions of anybody more inclined to argue politics, but also so dazzlingly compensatory for all of the party's myriad shortcomings that the surviving attendees would later swear they'd been lavishly wined and dined.

The Martha Stewart Paradigm, savior of beleaguered hostesses all over the civilized galaxy, was of course a trademarked patent of Shapiro Industries. And a good thing, too — since Dejah had devoted her life to suppressing dangerous technology, and the same basic software would have been fearsome beyond belief as a weapon of planetary conquest. After all, nobody can stand up against a war fleet with impeccable breeding.

Unfortunately, its programming was limited in one respect.

It was not capable of noticing assassin ferns.

The real Dejah felt a surge of cautious hope as she surveyed her handiwork from an invisible floating platform far above the mingling billions. "Okay, Karl. The plan's working so far. No disasters yet. Now we move on to Step Two."

Nimmitz peered over the edge of the platform, his puppylike eyes wide with boggled appreciation. "Wow. Step Two's further than Ernst and I ever got."

"I'm not surprised. Ernst usually had trouble getting past Step One."

Suspicion bubbled to the surface of his normally fathomless sea of incomprehension: "Are we talking about the same thing?"

She patted him on the hand. "No, honey, we're not."
And he turned red as a beet. "Oh."

"In any event," she said, "having given all these people

a reason to believe their social obligations met, I can now address myself to the even thornier problem of arranging their mass exodus off-world. Hmmm. There are far too many for cabs . . ."

"Even if they share?" Nimmitz asked.

Meeting his latest partner in crime aboard the mighty starcruiser *Jehosophat*, Ernst Vossoff was delighted to discover that the little lady was not quite so little after all. She was just a hair over six feet tall, she was as beautiful as advertised, and she insisted on being called Gwenda Black, which was far more pronounceable than her real name, because she hailed from Z'n'frrt'n'pkk, a particularly annoying planetary civilization of the sort that uses an indigenous language consisting of a long string of random consonants interrupted at random points by apostrophes. Since everybody who came from said planet had the same vocal apparatus as all other humanoid civilizations, they spent most of their days spitting into each other's faces as they struggled to pronounce each others' last names. Gwenda had naturally fled at her first opportunity —

"A good move," Vossoff approved. "I cannot even imagine how insane I'd be, if I had an apostrophe in my name."

"Could have been much worse, cutie. It could have been a hyphen."

Vossoff shuddered meaningfully.

Anyway, she fled at her first opportunity, rising through the ranks of the interstellar merchant marine until she was able to buy her own nano-fritter franchise. At which point, she said —

"My dear," Vossoff interrupted. "You are as lovely as a summer's day, and as charming as a sunset cast in shades of vermilion, and I would under normal circumstances be perfectly willing to endure your fascinating origin story until the custodial staff came out to clean up from the heat death of the universe, but I am postponing a long-awaited revenge here, and I really do wish you'd just get on with it. Specifically, who is this party guest who's worth so many credits if taken alive?"

Gwenda frowned. Looked aghast, as if she'd just swallowed something still capable of wriggling its legs on the way down. Seemed unwilling to believe in whatever it was.

And then leaned forward and kissed him lightly on the cheek.

"You know," she said, "you really are an adorable man."

Vossoff blinked repeatedly. "I am?"

At that precise moment, aboard Dejah Shapiro's palatial yacht, Karl Nimmitz was sulking.

He didn't sulk often; sulking requires an intellectual capacity sufficient to maintain the belief that one has been wronged. And Karl Nimmitz was the guy who had once nearly starved to death when a police officer who told him to put his hands up against the wall frisked him, judged him innocent, and walked away without first specifying that Nimmitz was free to go. Had the wall — itself a sentient creature manufactured by Dejah's subsidiary, Smarthouses Unlimited — not collapsed into rubble ten days later, out of sheer disbelief at the man's stupidity, Nimmitz might have remained standing there until starvation finally came to claim him. Sulking, per se, was usually more than he could manage.

Today, on the other hand, he had more than ample reason.

He thought his wife didn't appreciate him.

After all the trouble he'd gone to, just to throw her

this little party, was she grateful? No. She said a whole bunch of stuff about ecological disasters and millions of dead and ran off to run computer simulations of the best way to send everybody home without even a good global game of Pin the Indefinable Amorphous Extremity on the G'naaarg. She'd already spent so much time at the hytex consulting with her experts on a thousand different planets that she hadn't spoken a word to him in almost an hour. She hadn't even once asked him for his input. Of course, most of his suggestions were totally non sequiturs involving creative uses for pastrami, but he'd been known to come up with good ideas every once in a while — even if that was usually only in the relatively rare situations where pastrami qualified as a reasonable suggestion.

And the problem wasn't just today: the problem was their entire marriage. He never got to contribute anything in crisis situations. She was always the one crawling through the interdimensional phlux deconstructors to prevent the FTL drive from exploding, or tossing the slavering acid-tongued things out the airlock before they ate everybody, or neutralizing vengeful galactic warlords by negotiating peace treaties between armadas who had previously been at war for ten billion years. And somehow, whenever he asked if there was anything he could do to help, he was always the one directed to sit in a corner making little animals out of pipe cleaners. Granted that in all these years he'd never managed to produce anything more creative than various shapes of snake, it rankled. He wanted to be able to say that once, at least, he'd been able to do something to help.

So he sulked, and watched the monitors as they recorded how, on every single corner of the planet far below, the computerized simulation of his wife entertained billions of party guests simultaneously.

For a depressingly long time, his eyes were nothing

but little uncomprehending dots surrounded by little vacuous circles.

And then, on various planets throughout the known universe, the following things happened all at once: a star burned brightly in the east, iron turned to gold, a two-headed calf emerged from its mother speaking perfect Sanskrit, the fallen monoliths of Stonehenge abruptly righted themselves, the recently dead rose from their graves perfectly healed with no aftereffects beyond a slight lightheadedness that some among them attributed to too much caffeine, a Republican majority admitted that its major problem was simply not liking people, lost continents rose from the depths with all their treasures intact, and a publisher paid off its authors on the dates specified by contract.

Some observers called these events portents of Armageddon.

They might have been right.

Because somewhere within the space-yacht of his wife Dejah Shapiro, Karl Nimmitz's eyes suddenly flared with uncharacteristic intelligence.

He had just come up with another bright idea.

Meanwhile, on the planet Desiarnaz, the party was going as well as could be expected. Abraham Lincoln had sought out Thomas Edison, for instructions on how to program the VCR he wanted to set to catch the rest of *My American Cousin*; Orson Welles and William Randolph Hearst got sloppily sentimental about the old days and buried all their past resentments in a great big warm hug, promising to never ever let their differences come between them again; the Cro-Magnon who had first invented the wheel rolled around the party, trying to pick up chicks with his red hot cruising machine. Elsewhere, a delegation of politically conservative moths from the planet Znord had engaged a sentient parking meter from in a knock-down, drag-out debate on the evils of the flat tax; and several million people occupying the eastern steppes had organized a massive, frighteningly intricate game of Twister, complicated by the fact that the game board, projected onto the landscape itself by somebody's pocket hytex, was calibrated for some species that perceived shades only in the ultra-violet, and all the people playing had access to the comparatively limited human palette, perceiving the brilliant rainbow of mat as dull monochrome blobs which provided scant excuse for sensual contortionism. Meanwhile, on the other side of the planet, half a billion other people had gotten silly enough to take turns jumping up and down in unison in a misguided attempt to knock the planet out of orbit.

As for the fern, it was still doing what a fern does, which is absolutely nothing.

The man inside the fern was cackling evilly.

The determinedly energetic partygoers all around him were now engaged in a mammoth game of charades, that would probably last for a while since the phrase now being acted out by an overachieving ex-roommate of Dejah's was the complete text of *Remembrance of Things Past* by Marcel Proust ("7,322nd word, one syllable, sounds like *ear.*") They had any way of knowing that there was a man inside the fern. After all, he wasn't inside the fern in the sense of being physically contained by it; he was inside the fern in the sense of being completely encoded within its genetic structure. Thanks to modern technology and a very creative gardener, the essential building blocks of the man's being were not only safely stored within the leaves of this one otherwise unassuming plant, but his sentience and his emotions and his sensory input also remained fully online, experiencing the party via special simulation software that transformed him, at least within his own perception, from an inanimate plant completely devoid of personality to a devilishly handsome roustabout with blue eyes, rugged jawline, and a grin to die for.

This was, of course, an adjustment in self-image that many partygoers throughout the eons have been able to provide for themselves completely without the help of cutting-edge modern technology.

The man inside the fern utilized it only to keep him sane while he waited for his intended victim to pass within range. Sanity being, of course, an attribute best measured in relative terms. Because, measured in absolute terms, the man was about as stable as an ice-sculpture of an upside-down pyramid balanced on its point in the tropics.

He was crazy.

But he did have a bomb: not a round black ball with a long serpentine fuse that shot out sparks, not a dozen sticks of dynamite wrapped together with duct tape and attached to an alarm clock, not even a bunch of arcane circuitry inside a silvery metallic briefcase that could be defused by snipping either the red wire or the green wire, make sure you cut the right one, Mr. Bond. The bomb was, like the man himself, encoded within the genetic structure of the fern. It was designed to transform the plant itself into highly unstable compounds that could not possibly exist within the actual physical universe for more than a millionth of a second without an immediate, massive energy release capable of destroying everything in this entire solar system.

The man himself would of course also be annihilated in the blast, but that little observation did not factor into his plans, not because he was too nihilistically insane to care, but because he was too stupid. The fern was a pretty appropriate disguise.

Not that anybody would be around to compliment

him, when the bomb went off.

Which it would when his victim came close enough. Where was she?

There was, of course, one more complication that neither Vossoff, or Nimmitz, or Dejah, or Gwenda, or the fern reckoned on at all: a shadowy figure in a powdered wig, who stood ten meters away from the murderous potted plant, recognizing it, knowing exactly what it was, understanding fully the threat it posed, but waiting for his moment, and trying very hard not to hum.

It was a good thing that sound did not travel in space, because the lovemaking noises that would have otherwise filtered through the outer bulkhead of the Bettelhine Munitions warship *Jehosphat* were shameless enough to embarrass even the stars.

They were ninety very energetic seconds.

And when they were done, Ernst Vossoff and Gwenda Black were both collapsed in a sweaty heap near a storage bin near the warp drive, where all the spare pieces of the mangled space-time continuum were kept. Singularities popped in and out of existence all around their entangled forms, serenading them with various highly unlikely paradoxia; Vossoff, who'd needed to throw a shoe at an alternate-world version of himself to keep the pathetic loser from hooting, simply gazed at the beautiful young lady who had become the object of his adoration and whispered to her with uncharacteristic gentleness: "Your quarry. The one who's worth fifty billion credits if taken alive."

She brushed herself free. "Ernst, you romantic fool. Must we finish the exposition at a time like this?"

"Hey, I'm thinking of us. Even one-tenth of that money would be enough to buy us a garden planet where we can frolic in connubial glee for the rest of our lives."

"You're right," she said, nuzzling him. "It could. But what about the other nine-tenths?"

"Hey, you can buy the garden planet with your own money. I'm still entitled to my percentage."

"Ninety percent?" she said, frowning.

"And, a bargain at that. You do love my moustache so."

"That's true. It's those rocket fumes. It must be. But ninety percent?"

He kissed her lightly on the cheek. "Open to negotiation, my little hairy turtledove. I might throw in an extra couple of percentage points if you finish what you've begun. — No, not that. Tell me why this unknown partygoer of yours is worth ten billion credits if taken alive."

Gwenda sighed. "Oh, all right. His name's Krad Denacido. He's wanted by a certain interstellar banking cartel for fleeing their jurisdiction after losing ten trillion credits of their money on a bad real estate investment."

Vossoff stared. "Why would anybody invest in something as silly as real estate? There's more than we know what to do with!"

"Oh, back when Mankind was confined to one planet, people used to invest in real estate all the time. But since the advent of cheap interstellar travel, there have been so many worlds ripe for the taking that some restaurants give away planetary deeds as fortune cookies. But Krad invested in a ringworld — you know, one of those hoop-shaped artificial structures, hundreds of millions of kilometers in diameter, designed to rotate around a sun, providing more warm habitable land mass than a hundred thousand planets?"

"I've heard the concept," Vossoff said. "Again, why would anybody want to invest in such a silly eyesore?"

"Krad had the brilliant idea of using one to house the galaxy's entire population of snotty civil servants. After all, none of them are paid enough to make the rent anywhere else, and tucked away in one place like that they'd be easy to get rid of in one fell swoop if civilization ever figured out a way to do without them. Unfortunately, something terrible happened before he ever got around to moving them in."

"What?"

"It seemed that another real estate speculator named Rawlik had sunk all *his* trillions into a Pinky Finger World. George alone knows why. But he had this tremendous, habitable pinky finger a hundred million kilometers long, and he was transporting it to his home solar system for installation when. . . ."

Vossoff's tic had worsened noticeably. "Don't tell me. There was an accident, and the ringworld ended up encircling the Pinky Finger World."

"Unfortunately so."

"And I suppose the fit was perfect."

"Absolutely perfect. Too perfect. So perfect that the ring got stuck there."

"Ruining both worlds for habitation."

"For anybody with a modicum of good taste, yes."

"And why is this infernal loser at my ex-wife's surprise party?"

"To assassinate her."

Vossoff ruminated furiously. "Why?"

"Well, because she succeeded where he failed. She bought salvage rights to both worlds for maybe a tenth of what they cost to manufacture."

"Uh huh. And then —"

"She also bought the rights to an entire interplanetary civilization's output of warm soapy water, and . . ."

Vossoff stood up very suddenly. "That's it. I've heard

enough. I absolutely refuse to follow this any further. I don't need to go there."

"Constructing an equally voluminous bathroom sink world, she . . ."

Vossoff was jumping up and down in a tizzy. "I told you! I don't want to know!"

Gwenda seemed baffled by his behavior. "All right, all right. Calm down. Bottom line is that she made the quadrillions of credits that Krad and Rawlik should have made. Rawlik took it philosophically and got a job as floating swamp debris for some unlucky planet that had never evolved any of its own. But Krad, to coin a phrase, went mad. I believe he's come here to make an attempt on her life. The only problem with this, aside from the minor consideration that any injury done to Dejah will cause a recession of galaxy-wide proportions, is that he's making a suicide run, and if he doesn't survive we don't get our ten billion credits for bringing him in."

Vossoff ruminated furiously. "An interesting dilemma. However, am I correct in assuming that there's nothing at all preventing us from assassinating Dejah ourselves, once we've succeeded in rescuing her?"

"Nothing at all."

"Fine. Then that's the plan. We play cavalry, get Krad, claim your bounty, then indulge ourselves. — Tell me, do you have any recent description of the man?"

"I do indeed," Gwenda said. "He's a fern."

Thanks to the efforts of the Martha Stewart Paradigm, Dejah Shapiro's surprise soiree had instantly evolved from a disaster unmatched in the history of bad party planning to a scintillating evening dominated by the tireless charm of Dejah Shapiro at her most delightful.

Alas, the catastrophic devolution was just as sudden.

All over the planet, billions of previously contented Friends of Dejah gasped in appalled horror, overcome by the migraines that inevitably resulted from any serious attempt to maintain a coherent conversation with her husband Karl Nimmitz. In their minds, the charming and intelligent and personable and magical Dejah had just toodled off in search of fresh ice, promising to be right back — only to have her spot immediately taken by the coarse buffoon she had decided to marry. They were all obliged to listen to him, just to be nice to her, and they were all within thirty seconds or less knocked off their respective feet by pearls of stupidity that were to interesting conversation what massive clouds of superheated methane gas are to Chanel No. 5. The sum total of his various conversational gambits, ranging from the reasons why he didn't believe in Up to enthused tributes to the taste of wallpaper, inflicted upon every sentient being on Desiarnaz, constituted a faux pas on a planetary scale — all caused by his decision to appropriate his wife's advanced technology for his own party-mingling needs. Give him credit; he meant well; he thought he was helping. But the result was suffering and lamentation and gnashing of teeth on a scale never before seen, as all those billions hurriedly looked around for an exit.

Karl Nimmitz, watching all this from orbit, noticed the general increase in energy, but interpreted it as the party beginning to get interesting. Only the somewhat more laid-back annoyance of the fern, which the Paradigm program had relayed to Dejah's shipboard monitors, prevented him from believing that he'd just scored an unqualified success. It didn't matter to him that the reading had come from a fern; it didn't even occur to him that this was in any way suspicious or unusual. But it was cause for concern. After all, he was the host, and he wanted everybody to have a good time; if for some reason one of his guests was registering anything less than outrageous jollity, he wanted to know.

So he decided to go down to the planet and take matters into his own hands.

What could it hurt?

The mysterious figure in the powdered wig was still keeping vigil over the deadly assassin fern, still waiting for his moment, and still trying very hard not to hum.

Four hundred years earlier, and several hundred light years away, a (chronologically but not physically) much younger version of Dejah Shapiro lay blissfully asleep on sheets so soft and silky that the finest Earth-based satin would have resembled a bed of cat's-eyes and aggies by comparison. She slept alone on this particular evening, dreaming of Chocolate Heaven; and if her heartbeat occasionally raced like an out-of-control freight train at the thought of bonbons filled with 1-calorie creamy nougat, it also sometimes slowed down, to contemplate the more pedestrian pleasures afforded by the kind of cream-sandwich cookies which could be twisted to reveal the sugar-laced filling. Her canopy poster bed, which was as soft as a cloud and as wide as a football field, sat on a sea of immaculate white shag carpeting that was itself so deep and luxurious that servants and would-be assassins and lovers attempting to sneak out frequently got lost in it; there were rumors among her household staff that entire civilizations of such lost souls had risen and fallen without ever disturbing the placid, immaculately-vacuumed surface. Dejah didn't know; she kept a hovercraft parked at a dock near the foot of the bed so she'd never have to find out.

Tonight, the subsurface activity she couldn't see included a time-traveling Ernst Vossoff and Gwenda Black, hacking through the undergrowth in jodhpurs and pith helmets.

Gwenda said: "I can't believe this place. I think it sets a new record for conspicuous consumption."

"You should see her shoe closet," Vossoff grumped, as he stumbled over a waist-deep pile of lost contact lenses. "Even at this point in her life, there were enough high heels there to accommodate a synchronized high-stepping chorus line stretching from here to Aldeberan."

"That's a lot of top hats and fishnet stockings. Did you actually sleep with her in this room?"

"A few times, my pet. Alas, ours was the kind of marriage where I spent a large percentage of our evenings together exiled to the porch."

Gwenda was appalled. "In the cold and rain?"

"No. In the vacuum. This planet has no atmosphere. Oh, she was kind enough to give me a spacesuit, but she always shut down the only airlock after Midnight. I spent many a lonely evening breathing my air through the short tube connecting my suit to the front door, wondering just what little piddling felony I might have committed to drive her to such an extreme over-reaction, and unable to accept that it could possibly be something as insignificant as, let's say, shearing off her hair and selling it to highest bidder while she slept. It was," Vossoff said, shuddering with total emotional vulnerability, "before gathering himself together and moving on, "a painful time."

"You poor Baby," murmured Gwenda.

Vossoff slashed his machete into another vertical row of carpet fibers tall enough to blot out the sky, hacking them forty or fifty times more than clearing a path required, just from the sheer savage joy of it. "That's all right. I'm mostly over it."

"Then why did you set your ship for time travel and bring us here?"

"Because of the special stealth that defeating Krad requires. Think, Gwenda, think! Remember what you told me! As long as he's in this state, the man, the fern, the idiot, whatever you choose to call him, has a bomb hard-wired into his very genetic structure! We can't just wave a gun and disarm him! If we give any sign that we've penetrated his disguise, or make any obvious attempt to interfere with him in any way, he'll just set himself off and leave us the first but by no means last people at Dejah's shindig to grab hold of a superheated cloud of rapidly expanding hydrogen ions instead of a cocktail wiener on a toothpick. No, if we are to defeat this particular real-estate speculator, we will do so without direct confrontation — using a gambit that will first lead him to give up his herbal secret identity. And in all my centuries of unparalleled criminal brilliance, have encountered only one weapon capable of managing that particular feat."

He paused expectantly.

"What are you waiting for?" asked Gwenda, curiously. "You want me to guess?"

"Force of habit, my dear. Were you my doltish long-time partner, Karl Nimmitz, you would have used that cue to shout out something like 'Water Balloons!' Even after all these years of blessed separation, I still can't drop the habit of bracing myself for the mind-draining impact." He stopped before a looming pillar of polished wood, the width and height of a sequoia, rising through the dense thickets of shag carpeting to disappear in the mists high above. Vossoff smacked his lips with deep satisfaction, and said: "This is one of the legs of her bed. I will ascend alone, and return with the weapon we seek."

"Shouldn't I come with you?"

"I would not expose you to such danger, my sweet.

But if by some chance, while awaiting my safe return, you instead hear me screaming in terror and agony, and see my tattered form plunging toward you with a series of high-pitched shrieks along the lines of, let's say, Ohgodohgodohgod please please please get it off me get it off me get it off me, and you determine that I am indeed writhing in mortal combat with a hateful demonic thing intent on peeling the flesh from my skull, I will need you to do me one small favor before all hope is lost."

Gwenda had gone pale. "And that is?"

Vossoff, who had started to climb, shouted his answer down: "I will need you to shout *"Bad cat!"* as loudly as you can..."

Dejah Shapiro (present) sat at the console of her luxurious space-yacht, quickly and efficiently Solving The Problem. She had always been extremely talented at Solving The Problem; whether that problem was a simple hospitality question of what wine to serve with an elegant dinner centered around the incredibly rare and incredibly delicious red-meat fish of Norphus Seven, a creature who some thought had been genetically engineered specifically to irritate wine snobs who insisted that white was definitely inappropriate for red meat and red was definitely inappropriate for fish... or the far more uncommon conundrum of how to maintain an orderly existence when married to a man capable of accidentally stapling his tongue to the tablecloth at breakfast... Dejah always, eventually, knew exactly what to do. She'd solved the hospitality problem by using a lattice of semipermeable nanomembranes one molecule thick to segregate white wine and red in the same goblet, thus creating the galaxy's first, and to this date only, plaid vintage; Solving The Problem of her doltish husband had so far eluded her, but she could not complain, as at the very least it made life interesting.

In the meantime, she had worked out a way to send home the hapless guests at her surprise party. After running a high-speed search of the personnel records of her many enterprises throughout this galaxy, she had located and downloaded the personality profile of one Carlos Perez, who worked middle management at her Tracheal Keyboard Manufacturing Facility on New Omsk. Perez was a remarkable human being in that he had the uncanny knack of emptying out rooms faster than explosive decompression; whenever he reached into his jacket pocket and removed the hytex slideshow depicting his latest gala vacation to the integrated daiquiri vineyards of his homeworld, the exodus of bystanders who truly did not want to hear about it was said to attain speeds that could not be reconciled with general relativity. Dejah intended to use the Martha Stewart Paradigm, to inflict Perez on every sentient creature on the planet at once, while simultaneously using a wide-beam transporter to deliver Stargate Invitations to Unspecified More Interesting Places into the hands of all those billions who would now be overcome with the uncontrollable desire to leave.

She would have used her husband instead, but these were after all her friends, and she had no intention of inflicting permanent psychological damage.

The thought of Karl made her smile. What a sweet lug.

Then she realized that she hadn't seem him for a while, and alerted her scanners to report the conditions on the planetary surface.

Global panic. With him in the middle of it.

She was going to kill him.

The mysterious figure in the powdered wig had

hummed a little, without realizing it, but he'd shut himself up quickly; he still watched the Fern, waiting for his opening, knowing that if the day was to be saved, it was all up to him.

Four hundred years earlier, it had occurred to Ernst Vossoff, crossing a vast expanse of white down comforter that both literally and (for one who had been unhappily married to the woman who slept curled up in same), psychologically resembled the frozen Siberian tundra, that going to all this trouble to steal the weapon he needed to rescue her future self from a genetically-altered assassin in the shape of a fern, when he fully intended to assassinate her himself immediately afterward, could only be seen as a dictionary definition of wasted effort. After all, if he eliminated her, here in the past, he would not only have his much-deserved revenge, but he would also change a sad future history that ranged from transformation into a mountain of sentient fat to imprisonment inside a corrupt crime fighter's liver. Grinning fiendishly, removing his blaster from its holster, he tiptoed toward the distant sleeping figure . . .

Dejah Shapiro (past), still asleep, still lost in a blissful REM-sleep vision of snorkeling naked through a vat of primo milk chocolate Ghiradelli's, and too unwilling to surrender the infinite pleasures of that imaginary but still dangerously diabetic Xanadu in favor of the conscious knowledge that a sinister intruder was skulking toward her across several acres of mattress, was nevertheless also not caught without a Solution to the Problem. Without disturbing even one synapse of her waking mind, she sighed, shifted position, reached one hand beneath the white silk pillow, and emerged clutching a pearl-handled Lady Bettelhine Munitions Tachyon Accelerator Cannon with Concussion Grenade Launcher Attachment. In her dream, she skimmed the layer of double-chocolate fudge that masked the crunchy rice-crispy reef on the highly caloric sea floor; in the so-called real world, she triangulated the mysterious intruder's location from the barely noticeable jostling of her bed, leveled her weapon, filtered out the distant sound of Ernst Vossoff shouting, "No! *Dejah!* Stop! Don't shoot! It's me!," and fired at will. Even in her somnambulatory state, she possessed enough self-control to make this first volley a warning shot. The energy blast lit up her bedchamber like a miniature apocalypse, but made no noise other than a soft pat-pat-pat that resembled the restful sound of raindrops going pat-pat-pat against a sloping attic roof. Sleeping, cozy, at peace with herself and the world and the cartoony image of friendly caramel fish emerging from their hiding places to surround her on all sides in a veritable school of mouth-watering deliciousness, she half-smiled and slipped the Tachyon Accelerator Cannon back under her pillow, aware but not aware that the unknown threat was now receding, racing away in a great hurry in fact, and that there were simply oodles of hours of undisturbed dreamtime frolic still insulating her from the sharper-edged realities of dawn.

When the softly purring presence tucked against her ribs leaped to its feet and scuttled off, intent upon engaging in some nocturnal threat management of its very own, Dejah still didn't wake: but she did murmur: "Nice cat."

Four hundred years later.

Utterly failing to register the panic taking place on all sides of him, as billions of Dejah Shapiro's nearest and dearest friends from across time and space all attempted without noticeable success to run away from the billions of jabbering Karl Nimmitz simulations intent on driving them mad with cocktail-party banter composed of equal parts irrelevancy and banality, the so-called real Karl Nimmitz made his way through the maddened, screaming hordes to the side of the only party guest he had perceived as having a bad time. He knelt down beside the fern and began to tell the only joke he knew, which had something to do with a Vlhani, a Betelgeusian, and a Screaming Pylthothi Stink Moss all being stuck aboard the same crashing parachute with only one single-occupancy airplane between them. It was a terrible joke, and he told it badly, Nimmitz being the kind of guy who not only forgot the punchline, but who compensated by continuing the joke as long as he could in the hopes that he'd run across the punchline sooner or later. The fern didn't care; the fern was focused only on the awareness that its chosen target, Dejah Shapiro, was rapidly approaching.

In less than thirty seconds, it would explode.

Four hundred years earlier.

Gwenda, waiting at the foot of Dejah's towering bed, heard a sudden change in the quality of the screams coming from up above: they had been indignant before, but they were now bloodcurdling, so high-pitched they had entered the realm of sounds that could only be heard by dogs. She looked up and saw what resembled a previously undiscovered form of life plummeting toward her: a creature that seemed half terrified megalomaniacal Slav, half buzz saw. She recognized half of the conglomerate as Ernst Vossoff, shrieking the previously threatened getitoffgetitoffgetitoffgetitoff, the other half as the fattest, meanest-looking, most joyfully hostile calico cat she had ever seen, using its razor-sharp claws less as weapons than as valued investigatory tools in what seemed to be a thriving independent research project on the most efficient way a feline could enter a human being without using any previously existing orifice.

Uncertainly, she ventured: "Bad Cat?"

Four hundred years later: Dejah Shapiro's skimmer zipped low over the rioting party guests, racing toward the coordinates her ship's sensors had specified as the current location of her husband. The determined look on her face was a measurement of her intent to apprehend the poor dear before he further wreaked his own special form of disaster.

As brilliant as she was, she had absolutely no way of knowing that in this case, she was the threat.

Fifteen seconds now.

Somewhere in the space-time continuum, as the starship *Jehosophat* raced toward the last few seconds of the assassination crisis at Dejah's surprise party, Gwenda applied the latest in an endless series of synthflesh band-aids to the face of a grimacing Ernst Vossoff, creating from his visage a tableau that resembled a nose emerging from a sea of gauze. "I still can't believe that your big unstoppable secret weapon is a cat."

Between various grunts and moans, Vossoff traded baleful glares with the petnapped calico now regarding him suspiciously from an alcove behind the transmaat emitter. "Not just any cat, dearest. *The* cat. Sweetie. A creature less Animal than Aspect — the embodiment of everything in the slightest despicable about the feline character, which of course is everything. The hissing, shrieking, spitting epicenter of all maliciousness in the universe, a monster so selfish and perverse that only my shrewish ex-wife could have ever willingly taken it into her home."

Sheer affection prevented Gwenda from pointing out that the same description, omitting only the adjective "feline," could have been applied to Dejah's marriage to Vossoff. "You never got along, huh?"

"Indeed. The wretched beast was responsible for giving me more vertical stripes than an entire planetful of tastelessly upholstered easy chairs. But Sweetie hated one thing in this universe more than myself: the common fern. Whenever she found itself anywhere in the same ecosystem with a fern, it devoted all four of its brain cells toward tracking it down and reducing it to chlorophyll confetti. Dejah, of course, saw nothing inherently contradictory about filling the house with them. Some days, the freshly slaughtered mulch was ankle deep. — It is my belief that if we release Sweetie anywhere near our friend the homicidal fern, one of two things will happen. Either she'll shred it so quickly that it won't have time to explode, or it will activate some kind of genetic fail-safe designed to transform it back to Krad Denacido in the event of overwhelming danger. In both cases, the situation will be swiftly and painlessly resolved without requiring us to endanger ourselves."

Gwenda chewed on that plan. "And if you're wrong? If Sweetie's attack causes Krad to explode instead?"

"Then we lose Sweetie, Dejah, her oafish husband, and an entire planet filled with partying rich people. Which is a downside, but not much of one." He twirled the tips of his walrus moustache, flashed a grimace of the purest Stalinesque malignancy, and said: "And besides, it's the only plan we have . . ."

But this was not going to be one of those everyday

average ticking-bomb situations where the hero — or whatever Ernst Vossoff represented — was going to be able to swoop down at the last second to save the day . . .

The surface of the planet Desiarnaz had been reduced to a smoking ruin. Utter devastation stretched as far as the eye could see; the air was a smoky haze, redolent of sulphur and ozone and other compounds so noxious they could only be produced by a planet-wide cataclysm. Unrecognizable fallen forms lay in heaps across the landscape, also giving off smoke, their eyes wide and staring and eloquent in mute accusation of the fates that had brought them to such a final state.

This was, of course, just the normal aftermath of a poorly-planned party.

Had Krad's bomb gone off, the tableau would have been immeasurably worse.

Many of the partygoers who remained conscious after the moment of truth had already taken advantage of the Stargate Invitations Dejah had provided them to teleport into a smoky little after-hours club on a planet called Gr'nw'ch V'llge; conditions would probably be even more crowded there, since the club in question had an official capacity of only two hundred sentients, and the diehard revelers fleeing Dejah's party for more congenial fun spots still numbered in the hundreds of millions. So many of them teleported into such a small space that their combined mass congealed into a black hole, which nevertheless enjoyed the house band. Of those who sought out other venues, several hundred other million went out for pizza, and several hundred million others selected Dim Sum. Dejah herself went back to her space yacht to enjoy an hour of being moaned at by her insurance people — leaving only two partygoers still conscious, still standing, and still milling about on the planet surface to play dead dog.

Of those, one was Karl Nimmitz, who was standing by himself, humming a familiar song about Last Dances, when the air before him lit up with the familiar shimmer of transmaat teleportation. His face lit up with glee when he saw the first of the two figures who emerged: "Ernst!"

It was indeed his one-time partner, whose glare of furious incomprehension was one of the few facial features not swathed in synthflesh bandages. "The party's . . . over?"

"Pretty much," allowed Nimmitz. "But I'm still glad you made it! Did you have trouble finding the place, or what?" His puppylike gaze focused over Vossoff's head, at the pretty young woman with the calico cat in her arms. "Oh! Hi! Who's your friend?"

"Gwenda Black," the young woman said. As her eyes swept the landscape, it was clear that the limited nature of the devastation left her, if anything, even more uncomprehending than her companion. "Is Dejah . . . all right? I was a . . . college roommate of hers . . . don't look at me that way, Ernst, I was planning on telling you that eventually . . . but I heard a rumor that there was going to be some trouble here. . . ?"

"Oh, she's swell!" Nimmitz said, with enthusiasm. "If you're talking about that assassin fern, well, that gave us a couple of rough seconds there, but it all got taken care of, so . . ."

Vossoff was practically on the verge of exploding. "How!? How did it all get taken care of, you baboon? Did you —"

"No," said a man Gwenda and Vossoff hadn't noticed before, wandering into the conversation from around a heap of dazed guests in raccoon coats. He was short, slender, and dressed in a strangely anachronistic costume that included a waistcoat and a powdered wig.

"*You!?*" Vossoff exploded. "*You!?!*"

The newcomer preened. "Yes, I. I spotted that would-be assassin right off, immediately deduced that Dejah had to be the intended target, and spent the rest of the party, ever since then, skulking nearby as I waited for my opportunity to disarm him. When he seemed about to explode, I pounced and sprayed him with defoliant; this prompted him to revert to human form, both unconscious and ready to be disarmed. It was the least I could do for such a good friend as she."

Nimmitz said: "That's right. And then Dejah took Krad up to her yacht, so she could lock him in the brig. It was all really exciting, I don't mind telling you."

Gwenda, who was still holding the calico cat — which seemed to like her; the only thing that kept it from purring nonstop was the occasional hiss and spit it flung in Vossoff's direction — glanced helplessly at her fuming new partner in crime. "But Ernst . . . you seemed to know this man?"

"I know him all right," Vossoff spat. "He's one of Dejah's pet historical personalities. She collects them, you know. She met him when she traveled back in time to get him to compose a special march for our wedding. He deserves to fry in perdition for that sin alone, but for expecting me to accept this totally nonsensical, contrived, and totally unprepared-for last-minute rescue. . . !"

"What's the matter?" asked the man in the powdered wig. "Can't you deal with —"

Gwenda's eyes widened in terror. "Don't say it!"

"— An Amadeus Ex Machina?"

Somewhere in the universe, planets were colliding; stars were exploding; great blazing star fleets of warmongering overlords were pulling up to drive-throughs in order to ask directions. Some of these events may have been direct responses to the words just spoken on Desiarnaz. But it was impossible to tell. The silence that followed still rivaled that to be found in the vacuum of interstellar space.

It was finally broken by the long-suffering sigh of Ernst Vossoff, who rolled his eyes, shook his head, and declaimed toward the heavens. "I should stay here," he declared. "After all, I do still have a deadly vendetta to carry out. But somehow," he drooped, "after that," he drooped still further, "I'm just not in the mood."

"Neither am I," muttered Gwenda. " Take me out of here, will you, honey bun?"

Vossoff sighed. "Anything you say, shnoodle woogums."

And then they were gone.

As for Karl Nimmitz, he just stood there for a long time, his slack features a monument to incomprehension in all its myriad forms. It wasn't that he had any trouble dealing with his ex-partner's abrupt arrival and departure; he had dealt with Ernst Vossoff long enough to expect a certain amount of moodiness in the man. But this latest manifestation of the megalomaniacal Slav felt oddly incomplete. After all, almost all of his encounters with Ernst Vossoff ended with his ex-partner forever condemned to some fate worse than death; for Ernst to escape such an occasion with nothing but frustration was so completely at odds with the rules of the universe as Karl Nimmitz had come to understand them, that even his low-wattage brain was able to feel the impossibility of the moment.

He would not be able to completely reconcile it in his mind until Dejah came down to pick him up; at which point he told her what had happened, and she shook her head sadly. "It makes perfect sense to me, Karl. Ernst Vossoff is not your friend. He is not my friend. He is not anybody's friend. He is a sack of vice and corruption in the shape of a man, a megalomaniac and a sociopath and a fiend and a ravager of worlds and all-in-all not a very nice person. I divorced him. I transformed him into a mound of fat the size of a mountain range. I had him sentenced to hard labor on Ottoman 6. I once even got so mad at him that I performed a certain painful and time-honored trick with Crazy Glue. But even he doesn't deserve Gwenda. Gwenda —"

"Yeah?"

"Gwenda . . ."

"Yeah?"

"She's simply No Good For Men."

And Nimmitz, feeling the stars once again lined up in their proper positions, blinked several times in rapid succession. "Aw, gee," he said. "The poor guy . . ."

Somewhere in the universe, a once-formidable man sits in perfect darkness at the head of the stairs, his hands trembling like nervous doves in the space between his knees. It is too black in here to see what he looks like, but if the lights were to be turned on at this particular moment, his face would be revealed as pale, haggard, hollow-cheeked, and lined with the kind of stubble that is less a mark of another day's passage than the scar of another day's hell. He is shaking, this man: and any threat he once posed to the universe around him has been reduced to a ghost barely visible in the wreck he has become.

A voice cries out behind him: "Ernst? Honey? Come to bed . . ."

And as he shudders in dread of what must happen next, we gratefully draw the most respectful of curtains.

Epilogue

It had begun as a story told in a bar, and had proceeded without pause even during the runaway grease fire that had burned down the joint sometime during the bit with the alien coffee tables. Most of the other patrons had fled during the conflagration, some making it to their skimmers and rocketpads, others tripping on their own shoelaces and plunging into the swamp where they were devoured by Muzzleworms and Leeches. But she who told the story, and those who sat rapt listening to it, never stirred, even as the flames reduced their table to charcoal; never burned, even as a chandelier engulfed in fire plummeted from on high to smash that table to kindling. Not one of them was even singed. They were all protected, as all prop audiences are, by the Law of the Conservation of Narrative.

Now nothing remained except for them, and Dejah, and the charred and pitted jukebox, playing the obvious song by Jim Morrison.

The spit-curled alien goggled. "Just how long did this shit go on?"

Dejah smiled. "Indefinitely."

"He escaped again. Got screwed again. Escaped again. Got screwed again."

"You got it," said Dejah.

"How long?"

"For many more lifetimes. I haven't even gotten to the bad crap yet."

"Such as —"

"The time he got himself involved in a simultaneous time loop and cloning accident, and spent seven years slapping his future self in the face. The time he ran afoul of the mail fraud authorities on Clavin IV and couldn't get away until he first licked a postage stamp a thousand kilometers across. His year and a half spent inside out, tasting his own kidneys. The time he became the God of primitive natives who decided they didn't believe in him after all, and banished him to an old deity home. The time some unscrupulous surgeons wired his brain to the Clapper and chained him to a TV set so ancient situation comedies could turn him on and off. Hundreds more. All of them damnations beyond compare, spanning vast dimensions of space of time, all of them rescinded so he could twirl his mustache, plot more evil, and plummet headlong into the next punishment for his foolishness and greed."

The Pirate Alien grimaced at the devastation that surrounded them, rose from the dusty pile of ash that had once been his stool, took a step, and plunged into the gaping crater that had recently been the Men's Room.

Dejah winced as the shock wave from the impact took out of the establishment's few remaining unbroken glasses. "And to think I somehow avoided marrying that one."

The spit-curled alien wore the expression of a man who had just discovered unpleasant things about an orange substance in his underwear: i.e., simultaneously sickened and intrigued. "And he never quit? He never learned?"

"It wasn't up to him to learn," said Dejah. "The more it happens, the more I come to the conclusion that the entire history of the universe, from the Big Bang on down, was orchestrated specifically to create an Ernst Vossoff . . .

and contrive nasty positions for him. I don't know why, and I don't know how; I can only say that it couldn't have happened to a nicer guy . . . and that I spend every day grateful that poor Karl's destiny is no longer wedded to his."

She rose from the table, and headed for the door . . . only to be stopped by a single plaintive query: "Where is he now?"

She turned, flashed one of the greatest radiant smiles that had ever been flashed about anything not related to caramel, and disappeared out the front door.

There was silence, of a kind, until the jukebox began to play "Help!" by the Beatles. It was one of the few good songs in its carousel, which might have led the remaining barflies to permit it to remain unmolested for a few minutes . . . were it not for the improvised additions to the lyrics, which contained phrases as diverse as "Dejah, You Harpy!" "I'm in Here," and "Please Let Me Out." All of which clearly indicated a criminal lack of respect for the source material . . . especially since it was all delivered in a guttural slavic accent completely at odds with the intent of early period John, Paul, George, and Ringo.

The spit-curled alien was so distracted by all his unanswered questions that he limited his wrath to sinking it upside down in the swamp.

A Ridiculously Lengthy Afterword

I never expected them to develop, dammit.

That wasn't supposed to happen.

Of course, they weren't supposed to be a series, either. But that was a happy accident. Once they actually became the protagonists (if not the heroes) of an ongoing series, the evolution of the relationship between Ernst Vossoff and Karl Nimmitz was a royal pain in the ass. It became one of the banes of my writing life, and, aside from the death of their traditional venue *Science Fiction Age*, the main reason this series stands dead still where it is.

Stuff happened, is what I'm saying.

And not all stuff I expected to happen.

Look. Vossoff and Nimmitz are just two more specimens of a certain subspecies of science fiction story I happened to feel a little nostalgia for one day: the "two-guys-in-a-spaceship-get-into-trouble-*again*" story. I call it that, emphasizing the word "again," because the subgenre depends on repetition. Repetition is the whole point.

In this kind of series, two bickering guys in a spaceship repeatedly get into tremendous trouble and repeatedly have to reason their way out.

The fascination lies in the phenomenon that it keeps happening to them.

Ross Rocklynne wrote one such series in the 1930s, One guy was an interplanetary criminal, named Edward Deverel; the other was Lieutenant John Cobie, a cop dedicated to chasing him throughout the known universe in order to bring him in. The inevitable confrontation between this proto-Kimble and proto-Gerard was always complicated by the conditions of the alien environments where they met, which always trapped them in situations that forced them to team up. The most famous story in this series was "The Men and the Mirror," in which the pair topple into a gigantic concave mirror, sliding all the way down and then all the way up, dozens of times, losing sufficient momentum on each swing to know they'll soon be stranded, without hope of rescue, at the bottom. The solution has to do with recognizing their predicament as a form of pendulum. The physics don't quite work, but that doesn't matter. It's still a neat story, in part because it's only the most recent of several such confrontations the pair has had, and they operate with the unspoken assumption that the universe is going to continue fucking with them indefinitely.

Isaac Asimov produced his own pair of hapless guys in Powell and Donovan, spacefaring employees of U.S. Robots and Mechanical Men who couldn't go anywhere without the inherent ambiguities in robot programming forcing a crisis. In one such tale, "Runaround," they're stuck on Mercury waiting for a robot to deliver an important MacGuffin before their life support fails, and find themselves first required to figure out why the robot is gallivanting around in circles singing in verse. They solve the problem, of course — but in the very next story find the universe fucking with them again.

My all-time favorite practitioner of this particular

kind of story is Robert Sheckley. A substantial number of his stories (not the majority, by any means, but a few) feature Two Guys In A Spaceship Getting Screwed With By the Universe, and not always the same two — but he produced several about Richard Gregor and Frank Arnold of the AAA Planetary Decontamination Service, who like Deverel and Cobie, and Powell and Donovan, couldn't go anywhere without becoming entrapped in some absurd life-or-death situation that inevitably required an equally absurd last-minute solution. In one such tale, they stupidly equip their ship with a device that will provide them with anything they need — but only (they learn while well into their journey) once per item. Slowly starving, because the device includes food in its list of items no longer in stock, they come up with an elegant solution . . . one that nevertheless leaves them with an even thornier conundrum at the story's close.

Some folks will say Kirk and Spock are two guys in a spaceship. Well, yeah, they are . . . but though they behave like they're the only two guys on that ship, they're actually two of more than four hundred. To be a true Two-Guys-In-A-Spaceship story, the two guys must be a complete unit, like Laurel and Hardy, or Abbott and Costello. Just a pair of wacky guys who have the misfortune to continually find themselves in the wrong places at the wrong times.

The first Ernst Vossoff and Karl Nimmitz story, "Just a Couple of Sentients Sitting Around Talking," was mistaken by many for a Douglas Adams homage. Well, I can't say he had nothing to do with the madness that followed (certainly, anybody who noticed the dedication will have guessed that), but the first story, at least, was a conscious attempt to Do Sheckley. It is nowhere near as good as Sheckley, but by placing its characters in a Sheckleyesque situation and giving them a Sheckleyesque last-minute comeuppance, it nevertheless established what I was soon surprised to find out had become a popular and successful series running for much of the lifespan of *Science Fiction Age*. It helped that editor Scott Edelman found the perfect perennial illustrator in Joel Naprstek, who captured the idiot pair so perfectly that his vision for them began to illustrate the content of the stories.

By the time of the second story, "Just a Couple of Extinct Aliens Riding Around In A Limo," a tale I still consider one of the series' two best, the basic rules seemed to be set.

The titles would always begin with "Just a Couple Of . . ." and, though ridiculously convoluted, accurately reflect the story.

The stories would always end with Ernst Vossoff (the brains of the pair) and Karl Nimmitz (the kidneys) damned to some fate worse than death. There would never seem to be any possible means of escape, but the next story would write off their previous predicament as lamely as possible and set them up for another fall.

This, I felt, could continue indefinitely; guys like these could always find themselves a new fate worse than death, just as I could indefinitely produce some bullshit way to press reset and let them screw themselves again.

The series became less than consistent on a few matters. For instance, Karl Nimmitz, who is only mildly dim at its onset, becomes ever stupider as the series progresses, achieving some approximation of his ultimate single-digit IQ by installment three. You can attribute this to authorial fine-tuning, or you can say that his various travails leave him with progressive brain damage. (I prefer the latter explanation; when he gets a little smarter again, as he seems to in the "Strikebreaker" story, you can say that his neurons have had an opportunity to knit.) And though Ernst Vossoff is a small-time criminal at the onset, becomes a wannabe supervillain by the latter installments. I think the same explanation applies. In any event, the less-than-profitable relationship between these poor star-crossed fellas could have continued indefinitely without any noticeable change, were it not for the one monkey wrench that I ever-so-foolishly decided to toss into the gears.

That's right, folks. I provided them with their own personal Yoko Ono, in the form of Dejah Shapiro, impossibly gorgeous ex-wife of Ernst Vossoff.

I honestly thought I was being clever by sparing Karl Nimmitz a horrible fate for once. It played with expectations. It changed the pattern. It gave the series a new supporting character. It . . .

. . . like Yoko, ruined everything.

Although I firmly expected to do terrible things to Nimmitz again, pairing him with Dejah gave him something to live for, and thus rendered me loathe to inflict disasters upon him.

It gave Vossoff, who continued to get royally screwed by the universe, an increasing reason to plot revenge.

It split the pair apart. Rendered them mortal enemies.

Made the biggest challenge of starting any new Vossoff and Nimmitz story, not rescuing Vossoff (alone) from whatever horrible fate had befallen him in the previous installment, but also arranging some manner of sticking these two erstwhile companions in the same room together without immediately placing them at odds.

When the stories are read one right after another, the evolution is clear. Before Dejah, Vossoff and Nimmitz are inseparable. After Dejah, Vossoff hates his ex-partner with a murderous passion. Before Dejah, Nimmitz expresses misgivings, but still follows his partner's lead in all things. After Dejah, Nimmitz grows enough of a backbone to oppose his partner when necessary. The hostilities between these two erstwhile pals grows so very extreme that in the last two installments, they don't even meet except briefly...a state of affairs that didn't promise to get better any time soon.

They developed.

It happens.

But I sure as hell never expected it.

Where would the series have gone from here, if the boys hadn't been rendered homeless by the death of *Science Fiction Age?* The penultimate story, "Just a Couple of Subversive Alien Warmongers Floating All Alone In the Night," offers one clue. In that tale, having elbowed both of the men in her life out of the way, Dejah takes center stage for the first time. She turns out to be awfully good at it. I think she would have left Vossoff to this well-earned retirement as a Screaming Pylthothi Stink-Moss and taken over the series, with Nimmitz functioning as sidekick and comic relief. Don't be surprised if she appears again under these conditions. I certainly won't. Indeed, I even hope so. But I don't expect Vossoff and Nimmitz to pal around again. As a team, they're deader than Martin and Lewis.

Some other notes, for completists:

Ernst Vossoff and Karl Nimmitz make cameo appearances in stories other than the eight of their official canon.

They show up, for instance, in my X-Men/Spider-Man novel *Time's Arrow: The Present*, as lackeys of the evil alternate-world Cyclops.

They can also be spotted, unnamed but definitely present, in my Hugo/Nebula nominee "The Funeral March of the Marionettes." Remember the pair of bickering space pilots responsible for smuggling my protagonist Isadora to the planet Vlhan? How the story characterizes them as "Just a Couple of Incompetents With No Talent for the Work?" Well, that's them.

They will also appear, briefly, in a story still in progress called "The Box." (Now *that*'s a hell of a story, and if you don't see it within two years of this book's publication, get on my ass about finishing it, okay? Okay.)

As for the canonical eight:

". . . Sitting Around Talking" is the shortest and most embryonic of the tales. The boys don't seem themselves in this early adventure, and the universe seems too ordered to serve as their proper habitat. What can I tell you. They were still growing.

". . . In the Back of a Limo" is one of my favorites, even if Nimmitz shows an intelligence here that I soon began to pare away from him. It also introduces the Bettelhine Munitions Corporation, which was to become one of their perennial annoyances.

". . . Name that Tune" had the best Naprstek illustration of the entire series. Vossoff and Nimmitz staring in aghast amazement at the giant pink bunny. I want it.

The next tale introduced Dejah, but I like it anyway.

". . . Behind the Toilet Paper" was the last of the short stories; immediately after this one, the tales grew longer. That's probably because it was taking longer to get the boys talking to each other again . . .

". . . the Liver of Justice" was an attempt to introduce two brand new supporting characters; they didn't last long. The explanation of cellular biology turned out to be the highlight for most people, even those who didn't normally like the series. Some folks found Vossoff's fate, in the last paragraph, unbearably grim. Thank you.

". . . Floating All Alone In the Night" takes place on a version of *Babylon 5*. Its in-jokes include Captain S'Clri (a reference to fan Joe Siclari), who at one point says something "sternly" (a reference to Joe's wife Edie Stern). An alien race known as the Bursteeni (reference: writer Michael Bursteen) also shows up. The subtlest joke, however, is the "slightly bruised box-lightener," which I expected everybody to get, even if nobody did. This is my favorite story in the entire series, and might bode well for Dejah appearing again, someday, somewhere, sometime.

". . . the size of a planet" is a total, unredeemable mess; it makes less sense than any other story in the series, and is totally inexcusable. What the hell. That means you'll probably love it.

— Adam-Troy Castro

About the Author

Adam-Troy Castro made his first professional sale to *Spy Magazine* in 1987. Since then, he's contributed several other pieces to *Spy, Premiere,* and *The Quayle Quarterly,* and had a long-running column in the comics review magazine *Amazing Heroes*. His first published fiction, "Clearance To Land," winner of the first Jerry Oltion Really Good Story Award, appeared in the Fall 1989 *Pulphouse* Hardback magazine, and has been reprinted twice since. Another of his stories, "The Last Robot," was the first story in the first issue of *Science Fiction Age*. His novelette "Baby Girl Diamond" was nominated for the Bram Stoker Award, his novella "The Funeral March of the Marionettes" for the Hugo and the Nebula Awards, and his novella "The Astronaut From Wyoming" (written in collaboration with Jerry Oltion) for the Hugo and the Nebula Awards. "The Astronaut From Wyoming" also won the Analytical Laboratory Award, annually selected by *Analog's* readers. Adam has sold about sixty short stories in all, encompassing humor, mainstream, fantasy, science fiction, and horror, and including prominent contributions to the magazines *Dragon* and *The Magazine of Fantasy and Science Fiction,* and the anthologies *Deathport, The Ultimate Witch, Return To The Twilight Zone, Adventures in the Twilight Zone, Grails: Visitations of the Night, It Came from the Drive-In, 100 Vicious Little Vampire Stories, 100 Wicked Little Witch Stories, The Ultimate Super-Villains,* and *Skull Full of Spurs*. His original short story collection, *Lost in Booth Nine,* was published in simultaneous trade and hardcover editions by Silver Salamander Press in 1993. The author of the Spider-Man novels *Time's Arrow: The Present* (written in collaboration with Tom DeFalco) and *The Gathering of the Sinister Six* (first of a trilogy still in progress). He currently lives in Florida with two thoroughly psychotic cats who have been trying to kill each other since 1996.

Printed in the United States
885100001B